T0116977

Red Hot Holidays

Red Hot Holidays

Shelby Reed
Shiloh Walker
Lacey Alexander

POCKET BOOKS

New York London Toronto Sydney

Pocket Books
A Division of Simon & Schuster, Inc.
1230 Avenue of the Americas
New York, NY 10020

First Pocket Books trade paperback edition December 2009

POCKET and colophon are registered trademarks of Simon & Schuster, Inc.

For information about special discounts for bulk purchases, please contact Simon & Schuster Special Sales at 1-800-506-1949 or business@simonandschuster.com

The Simon & Schuster Speakers Bureau can bring authors to your live event. For more information or to book an event contact the Simon & Schuster Speakers Bureau at 1-866-248-3049 or visit our website at www.simonspeakers.com.

Designed by Akasha Archer

Manufactured in the United States of America

1   3   5   7   9   10   8   6   4   2

Library of Congress Cataloging-in-Publication Data

Red hot holidays / Shelby Reed, Shiloh Walker, Lacey Alexander. — 1st Pocket Books trade pbk. ed.
    p.   cm. — (Ellora's cave anthologies)
1. Erotic stories, American. 2. Christmas stories, American. I. Reed, Shelby. Holiday Inn. II. Walker, Shiloh. His Christmas Cara. III. Alexander, Lacey. Unwrapped.
PS648.E7R436 2009
813'.01083538—dc22
2009012768

ISBN 978-1-4391-4870-9

Contents

Holiday Inn

Shelby Reed

Prologue

J esse Proffitt stretched out on his son's bed, Daniel's
threadbare stuffed whale clutched to his chest, and stared
at the glow-in-the-dark stars glued to the ceiling.

They'd buried Daniel this morning, under a light drizzle
that had commenced three days earlier when a drunk driver
struck and killed him on the street in front of their house. A
hit-and-run. Daniel was chasing a neighbor's dog. The dog
made it to the other curb.

Daniel didn't.

Jesse tried to swallow, found his throat too thickened with
unshed weeping. Outside, the rain intensified and drove itself
against the earth, like his roiling grief. Even nature seemed
to know that a six-year-old so full of life and spirit wasn't supposed to die like this.

He was Jesse's greatest joy. His life. His world. Jesse couldn't think past the pain. It filled his ears, his nose, his eyes, his mouth, choking him. It bubbled and seared like molten lava in the center of his chest, eating his insides, his soul, everything except his heart, which had gone brittle and shattered into a thousand, free-floating shards.

And still the world was spinning in its callous, insolent way, when it should have gone still in reverence. Still Toni Braxton sang from the small stereo in the kitchen, begging someone to un-break her heart. She had a deep, rich, soulful voice that Jesse would recognize anywhere. Funny that amid all the pain, he could muse over Toni Braxton and her lush vocals. He wondered if she'd ever lost someone she loved to the black void of death.

Silence would have been more appropriate now that all the mourners had gone home, but Sheila couldn't stand the quiet. She never had liked stillness, so Jesse and Daniel had given her that damned mini-stereo last month for Mother's Day, and it never went silent. She was moving around the kitchen to its constant yammer even now, on the day she'd watched their son's coffin lowered into the ground.

The refrigerator door opened and closed. She was putting away the casseroles brought by well-meaning neighbors. She hadn't eaten a bite of anything since Jesse called her from a bystander's cell phone three days ago.

Sheila, come home . . . Daniel's gone. He's gone from us, he died in my arms . . . our boy is dead, and I couldn't even tell him goodbye.

Not that her inability to feed herself had much to do with grief, necessarily. She'd been too thin when Jesse married her a decade ago, and he'd long since grown sick of admonishing her to eat. It was a *thing* with her. Emaciation meant power. It also meant a bony, unyielding body curled away from him every night in bed. But the slow dissolution of their marriage hadn't really bothered him so much over the past few years, because Sheila had given Jesse a terrific son, the best friend a man could want, and Jesse could stand anything.

Anything but this.

On the kitchen radio, Toni Braxton sang about un-crying her tears.

He hadn't, yet. Hadn't cried. Couldn't. He'd stood at the foot of his boy's grave and held Sheila up, and her ninety-nine pounds felt like a thousand, crushing him. She'd wailed and Jesse had been her wailing wall.

Now he lay on top of their son's quilted cartoon bedspread and closed his burning eyes, breathing in the fast-fading scent of Daniel, the echo of his laughter, his husky voice shouting for Jesse to come kiss him before he could go to sleep. And Sheila moved like an automaton around the kitchen, straightening, cleaning, anything to avoid the bleak reality that remained, which included her husband.

The phone rang down the hall and Jesse's body gave a startled jerk. Soon the sympathy calls would quit coming, and people would move on with their lives, while Daniel Proffitt's parents sank in the quicksand of loss. No one could save them, not even themselves.

Sheila's voice, tear-choked, murmured over Toni Braxton. Inaudible words. A pause, followed by the click of her black high heels on the wooden floor, leaving the kitchen. Coming nearer.

"Jesse? Where are you?"

He didn't answer. She didn't need an answer. Her narrow shadow fed the falling darkness in the hall, and then she appeared, her face a ghostly white mask in dusk's gloom.

"Jess?"

"Yeah?"

"That was the sheriff's office." Her words quavered as Jesse sat up to look at her. "They arrested him."

"Who?" he responded automatically, even though he already knew. Even though Jesse's blackened mind had already decimated the man a thousand times in the last three days.

"The driver who killed Daniel."

He sat up to look at her, then said flatly, "All right."

When he looked up, the doorway was empty.

1

"So where are you, Anna?" Maggie Shea spoke around a mouthful of something crunchy, unashamed to munch in her older sister's ear over an already-scratchy cell phone connection. "Made it down through Rocky Mount yet?"

Anna glanced in her rearview mirror and maneuvered her Toyota sedan into the passing lane. "Not even close. Traffic's crawling. Drivers are road-raging. There's a reason why I hate traveling over the holidays, you know."

"But this is my first Christmas in my first house . . . Mom and Dad are going to be here any minute, and I can't handle them alone. You know how important it is that you be here." Maggie's voice rose in a plaintive fashion that sent Anna scurrying away from the argument.

"I know how important it is to you," she affirmed quickly,

"which is why I'm taking my life in my hands and inching two states through this godforsaken parking lot they call I-95. I wouldn't miss your party for the world."

"Or Christmas with your best sister."

"Or Christmas with my *only* sister."

"At least you have good weather," Maggie pointed out. "No snow, and you were so worried."

"So the weatherman says." Anna eyed the early afternoon sky through the windshield. One small cloud drifted close to the horizon in a sea of blue. "I just have a funny feeling about this."

"You do?" Alarm sapped the humor from Maggie's voice. "Is it a run-of-the-mill anxiety feeling, which would mean nothing, or a pit-of-the-stomach bad feeling, which would mean psychic intuition?"

"Strictly run-of-the-mill," Anna reassured, giving herself a mental kick. Maggie was so superstitious. "So I'll see you in about three hours."

"Call me every half hour so I know you're safe."

"You're a pain in the ass."

Maggie chuckled and hung up without saying goodbye— she'd always believed uttering those magic words would bring bad luck. Such idiosyncrasies had long ago ceased to unnerve Anna. Her younger sister's quirks made her lovable, if a little impossible. Her whole family was that way. Maybe that craziness was what had driven Anna to become a genealogist. She craved explanations for why the leaves of her family tree were so . . . colorful.

The party didn't start until dinnertime, and two hours into the drive, weariness strung tight bands across the back of her neck. She needed something to fortify her, pep her up, give her a jolt of temporary social enthusiasm, since all she really wanted to do was turn around and go back to Alexandria, Virginia, where her empty apartment and too-small artificial Christmas tree sat waiting.

Coffee would have to do, and a break from the stress of creeping along I-95 with all the other fools too entangled with their families to say, *No, thanks, I just want to stay home this year.*

It took another mile before a harried driver took mercy upon her and let her into the right lane, and with a sigh of relief, Anna swung off the next exit ramp and into a crowded gas station.

No parking spaces remained, so she pulled into an illegal spot on the grass, beside a dusty maroon Harley, and climbed out.

Despite the vibrant glow of the sun, the cold snatched the breath from her lungs. Icicles hung like crystalline fingers from the eaves of the convenience store, and customers pumping gas into their vehicles huddled against the wind's assault. The frigid currents shoved Anna along, whipping at the thin silk wrap she wore over her velvet minidress and loosening the pins that held her brown hair in its carefully crafted chignon.

Damn, but it was chilly. Whoever had the guts to ride the motorcycle she'd parked beside had a hide of steel.

Stepping into the warmth of the convenience store, she glanced around for the coffee machine and spotted it in the back. A tall man in full leathers and boots stood at the counter beside it, his dark head bowed as he doctored a cup of steaming coffee.

The motorcyclist, no doubt. Everyone else in the store was either elderly or weighted down with kids and junk food, moms and dads dressed in goofy Christmas sweaters and college football jackets.

Anna couldn't have explained why she hesitated in the entryway instead of heading straight for the coffee. The cheery store was crowded, Christmas music trilling under the steady hum of voices. There was nothing particularly scary about the man at the coffee bar, other than the fact that he was the proverbial biker—bearded, broad-shouldered and powerfully built. He probably wouldn't bite her if she walked up beside him and reached for the coffeepot.

When the glass doors behind her swung open and a blast of cold air stabbed through her clothing, she jolted from her rumination and forced herself to walk. The biker didn't look at her when she stopped at the counter beside him, but he did move aside to make room for her. Painfully aware of his dark presence, she poured herself a cup of coffee, and glanced around for the sugar.

He was blocking it.

She cleared her throat. "Excuse me. May I . . . ?"

He backed up a step and met her gaze.

Wild blue yonder. It was all she could think. His eyes were the iridescent color of the Caribbean Sea, made all the more electric by his dark beard and mustache, and the stern features they half hid.

An unexpected surge of sexual awareness washed through her as she reached in front of him and grabbed a couple of sugar packets. The scent of piney winter and worn leather emanated from him, and she quickly stepped aside again, surprised at her reaction. She liked clean-cut, polished, cerebral men who were familiar and utterly unthreatening. Grizzled bikers weren't her type. Unpredictability held no appeal for her, and this stranger's somber, fiercely blue eyes radiated it.

Maybe the lack of sex—a year's worth since her last breakup—had addled her brain. Or maybe it was just the idea of spending yet another Christmas as a single girl.

Somehow her relationships always met a tragic end just short of the holidays. It was a running joke in her family. Even Anna never bought her boyfriends Christmas presents anymore, because inevitably they would hit the high road by December 25th. And this year was the worst, because this year, for the first time, she really felt alone in the world.

So she gave her steaming coffee a slow stir and let herself indulge in the wayward pleasure of standing beside a man she didn't know. A mere five inches separated them; they stood too close, really, but he didn't seem to notice, and just the sheer thrill of breaching his personal force field pumped her pulse into a high, erratic dance.

A quick sideways glance told her his profile was more handsome than she'd thought, even with all that facial hair. She'd never kissed a guy with a mustache or beard. It might be prickly on her lips, too distracting. More likely it would be silky soft, delightful. It would glide a shivery path across the sensitive column of her throat along with his lips as he kissed his way down her naked body. Maybe when those lips found the curve of her breast . . . and then closed hot and hungry over her nipple, drawing on it, tonguing it, and that beard and mustache tantalized every inch of her aroused flesh . . . she would never want to go back to a clean-shaven lover. And oh, to feel the brush and tickle of that bearded chin on the tender flesh of her thighs, between her legs, and then the probe of a soft, wet tongue sliding down her cleft, savoring her, while his strong hands cradled her ass and lifted her like a loving cup . . . *oh my God.*

Pre-orgasmic shivers fluttered through her muscles, and she felt herself go wet beneath the velvet dress. How insane to get so excited simply by standing next to a complete stranger. Maybe she was having some kind of holiday mental breakdown.

Face burning, she stirred her cooling coffee one last time, then glanced around for a top.

The biker was, of course, standing directly in front of the stacked lids, and she wasn't about to reach past him again. Shouldering her purse, she started to turn away when he said, "Need a cap on that?"

His voice was low, quiet.

"Oh." She swung back and looked everywhere but at his face. "A medium one, please."

He retrieved the plastic top and handed it to her.

"Thanks." Delight quivered in her stomach as she stared at the front of his leather jacket, and out of sheer nervousness, she continued, "I can just see myself sloshing coffee all over this velvet dress."

"Going somewhere special?"

She glanced up at his gaze and away again, seared. Yep, those eyes were still blue. "A Christmas party."

"Have fun," he said without smiling.

"You too."

Jesus. He didn't look like he was headed anywhere fun. There was a starkness to his features that belied holiday cheer of any kind.

"Merry Christmas," she added uselessly as he walked past her. He might not even celebrate Christmas. It didn't matter. He was a stranger, a passerby in her day, no one she'd ever see again, although she would remember those gorgeous baby blues for a while. A woman didn't forget eyes like that. And if she ever had the guts to replay the intense sexual fantasy she'd conjured about that beard . . . it would definitely have to be somewhere private. Like in her lonely apartment, with her lonely vibrator, which probably needed dusting off by now, for all the action it saw. The morose thought stole the vague excitement lingering inside her.

She sipped her hard-won coffee without tasting it and watched through the store window as the biker climbed on the Harley parked beside her white sedan, slipped on his full-face helmet and rolled out of the parking lot. It was a sexy sight, a man straddling his motorcycle, sheer roaring power between his strong thighs, his face a mystery beneath the black-shielded fiberglass mask.

Only when the rumble of his motorcycle faded did Anna recognize the hollow sensation in her chest.

She felt as though she'd been left behind.

It took her a while to notice the dense clump of clouds that had dulled the glaring afternoon sun. She set her coffee cup in its holder and directed her sedan onto the interstate, where traffic had miraculously resumed moving at a pre-holidays pace. Spirits lightened by this heavenly phenomenon, she dialed Maggie for her thirty-minute check-in, dutifully reported her location and after hanging up, adjusted the radio to a festive slew of Christmas tunes.

That was when the first snowflake hit her windshield.

Glancing up in horror, she studied the fast-growing cloudbank and groaned as flakes drifted across the hood of her Toyota. How could this be happening when the weatherman had proclaimed Christmas weekend to be blue-skied and crystalline all the way down the Eastern seaboard? How, in this day and age of radar, computers and high-tech gadgetry, was it possible *to miss the gigantic storm* now brewing over North Carolina?

Within minutes the highway surface was wet and dusted with fine talc, and the heavens had turned to steel. Anna slowed her car to a crawl, noting with increasing anxiety that the traffic around her had thinned dramatically. People were actually pulling over on the shoulder of the road, hazards flashing their sense of alarm, unwilling to forge through what was fast-becoming the impossible.

A whiteout.

"No freakin' way," she muttered, and picked up the cell phone to dial Maggie.

An automated voice on the other end announced there was no available signal.

Ahead, red lights flashed as the pickup driver in front of her unexpectedly hit his brakes. Instead of slowing, the truck skated sideways and made a helpless, graceful slide into the grassy median.

Anna clutched the steering wheel with both hands, hunched forward to see the road, her heart hammering. The highway ahead was almost deserted. It seemed she'd moved into a foreign, cold, frightening land, where the only sign of humanity was the gentle tinkle of Christmas music beneath the roar of her heater.

Soon her entire world shrank to the two feet barely discernible in front of the car. No exits appeared. Nothing but hard-whipped snow, which clumped in the windshield wipers as fast as they could clear the glass. If this kept up, the blades would freeze and she wouldn't be able to see anything.

Anna swallowed the lump in her throat and tried again to call her sister, but it was no use. The storm must have knocked out a tower. Either that, or she truly had entered *The Twilight Zone.* Praying she wasn't overshooting the highway altogether, she eased into the right lane and took her foot off the accelerator in preparation to pull over.

Suddenly a pale red dot appeared through the miasma ahead, a ghostly neon orb that swayed and then shot hard into her path. She gasped and hit her brakes, slid a little and finally maneuvered the Toyota to a stop. In the dim glow of her headlights, a black-garbed figure lay in a tangled heap on the abandoned powder-coated highway, his motorcycle's rear tire still spinning.

Anna threw her transmission into park and leaped out into the storm. She couldn't tell if the rider was a man or woman; the black-shielded helmet hid his face. "Are you okay?" she called, slip-sliding with little aplomb to his side.

For a second the motorcyclist didn't move, and then he slowly pulled his legs free of the bike and sat up in the snow.

A man.

Hunkering down beside him, Anna brushed the white pow-der off his back and helped him pull off his gloves. "Oh God, did I mow you down?"

"No," his low voice was muffled. "I cut across your lane. I didn't see you." He unfastened his helmet and pulled it off, leaving his dark hair ruffled, but suddenly all Anna could see was a familiar pair of piercing blue eyes.

"Funny meeting you here," he drawled with no humor whatsoever.

She scrambled back, slid, and hit the snow on her bottom. "You're the guy . . . the . . . coffee . . ."

"Right." He raked a hand through his hair, straightened his spine, winced a little as he rubbed the thigh on which he'd landed. "We must be the last two fools left on the interstate."

"I was looking for an exit," she said foggily, her heart pounding.

"Me too. There aren't any."

"I noticed." Drawing a deep gulp of frozen air, she let her worried appraisal move down his long legs. "Are you okay?"

"Yeah." He got painfully to his feet, his breath puffing out in rapid clouds beneath the whirling snow, and offered her his hand. "Are you?"

"Oh. Yes." She grasped his fingers and allowed him to help her up, then quickly withdrew from his warm touch and backed up against the hood of her car.

The snow seeped into her velvet pumps as she watched him set his motorcycle upright. He was incredibly strong to handle the machine with such ease. Young, too, more than she'd thought the first time she saw him. And those amazing eyes . . .

The shiver that quaked her frame didn't have everything to do with the frigid air snaking beneath her thigh-length skirt.

He didn't appear to harbor the same romantic notions. After giving the motorcycle a once-over, he swiped his helmet from the ground and flashed her a solemn glance. "You should get back into your car where it's warm."

"I'll wait to make sure you get safely on the road."

With a shrug that said *suit yourself,* he pulled on his helmet, flipped down the face shield and straddled the bike.

"Take care," his voice came muffled at last.

"You too." She picked her way around to the Toyota's driver's side, shaking hard from the cold and excitement. Any second and the roar of his bike would fill the air, he'd ride off and she'd never know why their paths had crossed.

Hell, who needed a reason? She sounded like Maggie, searching for keys to the universe. Maybe the insanity was genetic after all.

Inside the car, Anna pulled on her seat belt and cranked her heater, all the while taking guilty pleasure in the sight of the biker's strong form straddling the motorcycle as he tried to start it.

And tried. And tried.

Her pulse jumped in her veins, a wayward thrill tickling her nerves. Frustration wrote itself in every lean line of his body as he attempted again and again to start the Harley, and failed.

His bike was dead. She couldn't leave him stranded out here in the middle of a blizzard.

She couldn't take him into her car, a dark, unpredictable stranger.

The motorcycle fired finally . . . and sputtered out. His head dropped forward in abject frustration. And all the while, Anna's heart performed impressive acrobatics, because it had already made the decision for her.

He dismounted, kicked down the stand and stood with his hands on his hips, studying the Harley. After a minute, he gave its exhaust pipe a scolding nudge with the toe of his boot, then gathered his backpack and trudged over to her car door.

Butterflies swooped and soared in her stomach as she lowered the window expectantly.

"I hate to ask you to do this," he said, leaning low to meet her eyes through the full-face helmet, "but—"

"Of course."

"Just to the nearest exit."

"No problem."

And hitting the unlock button, she invited him in, a dark, bearded stranger with the bluest eyes she'd ever seen.

2

Anna drove at a snail's pace through the storm, her fingers clenched and sweaty on the steering wheel, every muscle in her body tight with awareness of her silent passenger.

When she stole a glance at him, he was staring out the window, one elbow resting on his helmet, his forefinger stroking his mustache. He seemed to be somewhere else, and not one bit interested in making her acquaintance, which should have been a relief.

It wasn't. The scent of leather, male exertion and melted snow filled the car's interior, stole her common sense, plucked at a female place deep inside her that made her want to lean across the console and bury her nose in his short, tousled hair. He was all male, impenetrable, a rock. Under those smooth-fitting black leathers no doubt dwelled all kinds of lean, hard delight. But beyond the physical allure, he radiated a strange melancholy and a raw sensuality that was as frightening as it was appealing.

He wasn't her type. She was nuts to want him, yet she did. So much that she could barely sit still beside him. Her mind played tricks on her, flashing images before her eyes that were carnal, outlandish and wholly reckless considering her focus needed to be on the icy road.

Lost in the sheets of some generic fantasy bed, she would let him toy with her, tease her with slow, circling thrusts, let him rub against her until she shuddered and came, and came again. Then, when enough was enough, she would clutch his damp back, roll him over with wild strength granted by lust and sit astride him, her hair loose and tangled as it thrashed her breasts in time to her movements.

"Faster," he'd order, his hips pushing hard beneath her so that she rose high, impaled on his steely cock. Instead of obliging him, Anna would pin his broad wrists to the mattress and slow the enticing rotation of her pelvis. He could only touch her when she allowed, even though every grinding slide of her sex against his hard shaft threatened to dissolve her power and render her mindless and vulnerable.

But it was her fantasy, and she was a siren, capable of wringing helpless cries from even this dark, dangerous man. After an agonizing forever, after perspiration dampened their bodies and his legs slid against the mattress in restless agony, after his harsh exhalations had turned to low groans and his hands twisted in the sheets . . . she would reach behind her, let her fingers find the sensitive sac beneath his cock and fondle him, and the tender flesh would tighten like magic beneath her skilled caress, a harbinger of the impending explosion.

"Fuck me," he'd growl, his dark head thrashing on the pillow. "Fuck me hard, Anna—do it now!"

And with her own orgasm simmering like hot oil in her belly, she would free him, ride him fierce and fast, revel in the hard slap of flesh meeting flesh, the rising commingled scent of their desire, the rising song of their ecstasy, until every muscle in his strong, sweat-slicked body tightened and bunched, and he churned out pulsing jets of fire within her. While he was still quaking, still calling her name, she would soar to the sky, crest and fall into a hundred tiny deaths of sanity. The aftershocks of her orgasm would milk him until he sank into the mattress and she fluttered like a fragile leaf atop his strong body. Then he'd stroke her damp hair with all the tender gratitude of a sated lover, kiss her temple, and say—

"How about now?"

She visibly jerked and embarrassment scalded her cheeks. "I'm sorry?"

"There's an exit coming right up." He turned his head to study her.

Anna swallowed and stared at the road. "I didn't see the sign."

"There were two of them," he offered, and when her gaze darted back to him, he was regarding her with grave intensity. God only knew how much of her thoughts were written on her burning face.

"Well, thank God." She maneuvered the car carefully onto the exit ramp and crept to a stop sign half buried beneath ice and snow. "Do you have any idea where we are?"

"Nope. There's a gas station." He gestured to a faded blue and red billboard, but when they rolled by the station, its windows were boarded up and tall brown weeds poked through the abandoned snow-coated lot.

Anna's unease tightened into trepidation. Where *was* everyone? They couldn't be the only two people out in this freak storm. Where had the rest of the world gone?

In the distance, a row of golden lights sparkled through the blowing collage of white. "A motel!"

"That'll do," he said.

Minutes later the Toyota pulled in front of "Holiday Inn," only this motel didn't belong to any giant hospitality corporation. It was a one-floor motor lodge, circa 1960, with a green and red retro façade and snow-frosted gables. Anna was comforted to see the variety of vehicles parked in front of the rooms. She and the biker weren't the last surviving life-forms in the universe, after all.

A rotund, bearded man dressed in Christmas red—complete with plaid suspenders—waddled down the walkway with towels under his arm, and gave them a cheery wave as he passed.

"Merry Christmas! Come in out of the storm!" he called, before disappearing inside a room.

Anna smiled and turned to her passenger. "Maybe you can call someone to pick you up here, or . . . or . . . ?"

"Yes." He didn't say who that someone would be . . . a wife? Girlfriend? Before Anna could cross the line into nosiness and ask, he reached across the console and touched her elbow. Just a brush of fingertips, but she felt it down to her marrow. "Thank you for the ride."

"You're welcome," she replied breathlessly as he climbed

out into the waning storm. It seemed so abrupt, their parting. So sudden, like something had been left unresolved.

Oh, well. That was it. The adventure was over, the stranger gone, her foray into reckless behavior ended. A snowplow rolled by the motel on the two-lane highway, headed for the interstate. She could get back on the road now, and spend the next one hundred miles mooning over what could have been with that sexy, forbidden stranger if she'd had even *one ounce* of raw courage . . .

Her sister had won the guts lottery in the family, however. And Maggie was going to love this story of the one-night stand that never was.

Anna made it to the interstate ramp and braked to dial her sister's number. Still no signal. If the storm continued to abate, she would only be a little late for the party. The Toyota revved a high squeal when she accelerated.

"Oh, no, you don't," she muttered, shifting gears. In reply, the car jerked and sputtered, made an ungodly sound she could never describe to any mechanic . . . and shut off.

"No, no, no! Shit, shit, *shit!*"

No amount of coaxing could get the engine to turn over. Tears lodged in her throat, she hit the hazard button, climbed out and stood in the middle of the deserted ramp beside her lifeless sedan. What the hell was she going to do now? Not a soul was in sight, not even the snowplow, which was just as well, since her dead Toyota was sitting smack in the center of the road.

It was a long, cold walk back to Holiday Inn, and by the time she reached the office, her feet were screaming in their soaked velvet pumps and her nose was so cold, she wasn't sure it hadn't fallen off her face. Every muscle was rigid from shivering, and when she stepped into the golden warmth of the tiny, wood-paneled lobby, she got as far as the nearest plaid sofa before collapsing.

"It's a nasty one out there, eh?" The jovial voice from behind the counter startled her into an upright position. She hadn't seen the clerk when she walked in, but suddenly there he was behind his wood-paneled station, white beard, bald shining head, dressed in a red-and-white-striped shirt and those crazy plaid suspenders.

Santa Claus, Anna thought dazedly as she got to her feet. How *apropos.*

"What brings you out in such a storm, my dear?" he asked, much too merrily for her current mood.

"My car has stalled on the interstate ramp," she told him in a carefully restrained voice. "Do you know of any nearby service stations that could help me?"

He rubbed his whiskered chin. "Not this late on Christmas Eve."

She closed her eyes, drew a deep breath for strength. "How about a room, then?"

"'Fraid we're all full up for the night. Lots of travelers thrown by this freak storm." He nodded at the large picture window. "It's coming down again, harder than before."

He didn't have to be so cheerful about it. Anna wasn't one for weeping, but the urge to do so, and do it loudly, surged in her chest and suffocated her response, which would have been, *You've got to be shitting me.*

"We're 'bout to close up here, go home to our families," the happy little man continued, as though they were sharing a congenial fireside chat. "How about you? Are your loved ones close by?"

She shook her head, self-pity choking her ability to speak.

"That's too bad. I'd like to let you stay here in the lobby, but I'm off the clock now, and I've got orders to lock up for the night. Cash register and all, you know. You can use the phone here to call the highway patrol though. Maybe they can help."

Hell of a Santa Claus he'd turned out to be. Resisting the urge to tell him exactly what she was thinking, she dialed the number on the old-fashioned rotary phone with stiff fingers, and when the highway patrol dispatcher told her it might be morning before a patrol car could reach her, *". . . what with the storm slowin' things down and lots of accidents ever' where . . ."* Anna knew there'd be no Santa this year.

"Thank you," she called to the little man, who had disappeared into a back room. *Not that he deserved it.*

He poked his bald head around the doorway, his blue eyes twinkling. "May your Christmas be filled with magic, dear."

"Same to you," she gritted, tears stinging her eyes. Frankly it was the thought of hiking the half mile back to her car that grieved her, even more than spending a frigid, blustery night— Christmas Eve!—in a car with no heat.

In thirty years, she'd never felt more alone.

3

Jesse ran warm water in the sink and let it pour over his fingers, soaking in its comforting heat, letting his weary mind drift, if only for a moment, away from reality. He hadn't felt anything but sadness in so long, and the acid of grief had eaten holes in his brain, through which his thoughts seeped, disjointed and agonized.

But there had been a single breath of clarity, of normalcy, today of all days. The pretty brunette in her tin-box Toyota, all wrapped up in silk and velvet like the sweetest Christmas gift. The tenderness about her, the endearing clumsiness, the kindness in her big brown eyes, the sexy way her swan neck flowed into her graceful shoulders. The curve of her breasts beneath that wacky, useless shawl she wore, as the relentless wind whipped her chestnut curls free from her fancy hairdo.

He'd wanted her. The realization struck him now, brought

a rueful smile to his lips as he stared down at the steaming water trickling over his fingers. *I guess you're not as dead as you thought you were.* In another lifetime, he might have had the balls to ask for a parting kiss from such a beautiful woman. A brief taste of her full, sensitive mouth would have lifted him up and out of the bleak movie his life had become. And it wouldn't have been so out of place to ask for a kiss. For a while, they'd shared an adventure. Two strangers whose paths had intersected not once, but twice—and while Jesse didn't believe much in fate, the scenario certainly offered some interesting possibilities to his writer's imagination.

But he hadn't asked to kiss her. Hadn't even thought of it until now. One more missed opportunity, and normally he didn't care. Tonight, though, it mattered. He regretted the way they'd passed through each other's lives. Even now he could picture her moving among the guests at her party tonight, sipping champagne, smooching cheeks, shaking her sweet backside beneath that short velvet dress to some sultry beat on the dance floor.

That tugged his mouth up into a smile, but when he caught his reflection in the mirror, the pleasure faded from his bearded features. He hardly recognized himself anymore. How had he come to this? People lost children every day and moved on. Why couldn't he? Why had he lost everything when he lost Daniel? His entire life—his writing career, his marriage, his home, his identity—slipping away like the water gliding through his fingers.

He'd let it all go without a fight, except for Daniel's ghost. It was killing him, day by day, pulling him out of this world and into another where nothingness reigned. He was drowning, letting himself drift further and further from recovery. He had become a ghost himself.

The water in the sink abruptly went cold and he straightened, shutting off the spigot. A coffeemaker sat on the counter to his left, but he didn't want coffee. He needed something stiffer. Whiskey. A tiny flask was tucked inside his backpack for occasions such as this, when the nights got too long and his isolation too profound. He'd never been much of a drinker, but at this moment it promised a welcome escape.

He loosened the flask's lid, then hesitated. The bitter medicine might go down easier with a little cola, and maybe he'd sleep for a while, his only break from the pain that drove him. He'd passed a soda machine near the motel office, although there was no guarantee it would work. Everything about the tiny motor lodge seemed lost in time. Just like he was.

Retrieving a handful of coins from his jacket, he opened the door and stepped out into the covered walkway, just in time to see a slender, familiar figure limping away from the motel and into the wind-whipped parking lot.

"What the hell . . . ?" Hunching against the blowing snow, he jogged after her. "Hey!" *Christ, he hadn't even asked her name.* "Miss!"

The heavy precipitation swallowed his call. Only when she paused to adjust her thin, soaked shawl did his voice reach her, and her head shot around, her fawn eyes wide and liquid with tears, wet strands of chestnut hair frosted with ice.

She was shivering. Crying. An unnamed sensation fisted around his heart as he reached her. Without thinking, he folded her into his arms to protect her from the swirling storm, and she didn't resist.

He meant to ask her what she was doing—was she *crazy*?—but she melted into him just right, as though she belonged in his arms, and only when the wetness of her garments soaked through his shirt did he pull back to meet her brimming eyes.

"What the hell are you doing out here?"

"Hugging a stranger?" She laughed, but it sounded choked. "After I dropped you off, I thought I could get back on the highway. The storm was letting up. I mean, it appeared to be. I'm not crazy enough to get back on the road in a blizzard. But—you saw that the storm had let up, right?"

"Sure," Jesse said, his embrace absorbing the hard shudders of her body. She might be a little nuts, but she smelled like a rose in winter, soft and rich.

"I barely made it to the on-ramp and my car died," she was saying. "No warning. There's nothing wrong with that car, I'm telling you. I take such good care of the cheap piece of junk! And it flat-out died!"

"The nerve of it," he murmured, knowing she wasn't listening as she clung to him, her words coming in warm exhalations against the bare skin where his collar fell open.

"And then the snow just poured on my head like someone had dumped a bucket of ice on me, and—and I walked back here, but there are n-no vacancies."

"I took the last room." He cursed under his breath and tightened his embrace, his chin finding the top of her head. It felt too damn good to hold this woman, standing like a crazy man with her out in the storm.

She was sobbing now, her shoulders heaving, whether from the cold or the tears he didn't know. "It's not your fault. Ugh,

look at me. Normally I don't do this. It's just that . . . it's C-
Christmas—"

"Come on." He started to lead her toward his room, but she
stiffened and withdrew from his guiding arm.

"What are you doing?"

"Taking you somewhere warm."

"Your room?"

"The office looks locked up and closed," he said. "Do you
have a better place in mind?"

She bit her lip. "I don't know you."

"No, you don't," he replied, shivering himself now. "But I'm
not about to hang out here and freeze to death just to let you
get better acquainted. You want to come in or not?"

She lifted her chin and studied his eyes, her teeth chatter-
ing. "Fine. I'll accept your offer as a return favor for helping
you on the highway. Only until the snow lets up and I can call a
tow truck. And no funny stuff."

"Speak for yourself," he pointed out, poker-faced.

Her head tilted in consideration. "Well, true. I could be a
serial killer for all you know."

"Maybe you'll have mercy on me and take a break from all
that violence. After all, it's Christmas Eve." And when at last a
smile twitched on her delectable mouth, he led the way into
his room and shut the door behind them.

Despite her bravado, unease swirled around Anna as unrelent-
ing as the blizzard's wind. Here she stood inside a stranger's

room, staring at him, and he at her, his bright blue eyes giving nothing away. And outside the world had disappeared in a miasma of white fury.

If this man wanted to hurt her, he could easily have his way. He was, as she'd earlier suspected, strong-limbed and lean. He'd shucked off his leather jacket. His plaid flannel shirt stretched taut across his broad back as he finally moved, leaned to pick up the ruined shawl that had slipped from her shoulders and hung it in the tiny closet to dry.

"I was going to make myself a drink," he said, his voice quiet in the room's hush. "Would you like one? I can grab you a soda from the machine."

"That would be great." Still quaking from the cold, she eased down onto a worn wingback chair and squeezed her chilled hands between her nylon-covered knees to warm them.

He disappeared outside again, and she sat in utter stillness, shell-shocked by the unbelievable reality of this day. She no longer felt like crying. This was all too interesting to give into despair just yet.

After a moment she retrieved the phone from her wet purse and dialed Maggie's number. This time the call went through, and for a moment hope swelled in her heart. But there was no answer; not even the machine picked up. She dialed again, to no avail.

The entire day was beginning to feel like one fat cosmic joke.

The biker reentered the room, two soda cans hugged against his chest. Snow dusted his dark hair, and he shook it off like a big dog and shut the door with his foot.

"It's bad out there," he said, and leaned behind Anna's chair to crank the heating unit, close enough for her to study the smooth seat of his leather pants.

He had a nice ass, she managed to note through her misery. Muscular, but not the bulky bubble-butt of a weight lifter. His physique was obviously compliments of Mother Nature. So was the easy way he moved, with enough liquid ease to indicate innate sensuality—half the reason for Anna's discomfort. She might not trust him, but she trusted herself even less. Desperation did funny things to a woman's code of ethics. Right now she could hardly remember what her mother had taught her about strangers and motel rooms with only one bed.

Outside, the wind wailed a mournful elegy, but warmth had begun to return to Anna's limbs, and since the biker had retreated to the bed and seemed to be keeping his distance, she relaxed a little.

"Before you even think it, I don't plan on getting wasted." He retrieved a small flask of whiskey from his knapsack and splashed a finger into a glass on the bedside table. "I just want to warm up, and I'd suggest you do the same."

"Plain soda, please," she said stiffly. "I'd like to keep my wits about me."

If he was insulted by her obvious doubt of him, he didn't show it. After he'd handed her a glass of cola, he finished making his drink. Then he sat down on the edge of the queen-sized bed with the glass cradled in his big hands and wordlessly met her gaze.

Anna swallowed a mouthful of cola and glanced away. His eyes were so clear, so piercing, like the azure marbles she'd collected as a kid. She wanted a longer look at them, but they stung her. "What's your name?" she asked finally.

"Jesse." His lashes lowered as he studied her mouth. "You?"

"Anna."

He lifted his glass in her direction. "To being stranded in the middle of nowhere on Christmas, Anna."

"Cheers," she echoed, and took a long gulp. Silence blanketed the space between them, and underneath, an unnamed tension roiled and flowed. After a beat, she said, "You know, Jesse, I think I will have a little whiskey with my soda."

He obliged her, then returned to his post on the edge of the bed, and they finished their drinks without speaking. Outside, the storm raged, and soon the lateness of the afternoon swallowed what remained of the frail, frozen daylight. Jesse reached over and turned on a bedside lamp, filling the room with a soft golden glow.

Thawed at last by the whiskey, Anna kicked off her ruined pumps, curled her feet beneath her and sank deeper into the chair's winged embrace. Despite the strangeness of the situation, it was damned good to be off the highway. Weariness weighted her eyelids, and she forced them open again, not quite secure enough to sleep in this man's presence.

Without a word, he rose and withdrew a blanket from the closet, tossed it to her. Keeping his distance, even though less than an hour ago he'd wrapped her in his arms and she'd come more than willingly.

"Thank you," she murmured, and the words held a deeper import.

He gave a short nod. "I'm going to sleep for a while."

She tensed again, her gaze following him as he pulled back the covers and threw one pillow to the foot of the bed. He didn't offer to give her the bed and he didn't offer to share it.

He pulled off his boots, tugged his shirt free from the waistband of his pants and stretched out on the mattress.

"Wake me if you need anything," he said, and just like that, he fell asleep, leaving her in peace, wholly surprised, and inexplicably disappointed.

While he slept, Anna crept into the bathroom, locked the door and ran herself a hot shower. She hung her soaked clothing up to dry and stepped beneath the steaming spray, where she lingered until the water went tepid. When she was done, she wrapped herself in a towel and sat on the toilet lid, unsure of what to do next. It wasn't appropriate—or smart—to flounce around the room in nothing but a towel while her clothing dried, even if the biker wasn't awake to witness it. On the other hand, she couldn't sit in the tiny, steam-filled cubicle all night. Gritting her teeth, she put her clothing back on, which no longer was drenched, but merely damp and icy to her tender skin. It was hell, but at least she was clean and somewhat thawed.

Shivering, she eased the bathroom door open and tiptoed into the room. The biker had changed positions on the bed; he lay on his side away from her, silent, the steady rise and fall of his back indicating he truly was asleep.

He looked cold.

Moving stealthily, Anna drew the side of the bedspread over his huddled form, then backed away to watch him, half frightened, a quarter miserable, and the rest . . . well, titillated. Knowing that nothing would happen between them gave her love-hungry mind free rein to entertain a million erotic scenarios. *Two strangers, both solitary, stranded in a storm, sharing a motel room with one bed out of sheer desperation. And sheer desperation would ultimately drive them together.*

Sounded like a movie . . . a juicy one.

She groped for the chair behind her, curled up on it, and covered herself with the blanket he'd offered her earlier. After a while her thoughts slid into a sleepy collage of fragmented fantasies, and finally, dreams.

Anna didn't realize she'd dozed off until the sound of water rushing through creaking pipes roused her back to life.

The bed was empty, the covers rumpled. From the bathroom came the sound of a shower running, the thud of soap hitting the tub floor. After a minute the water shut off, followed by the clack of shower curtain rings sliding on a metal rod.

He was in the shower. Naked. With one thin wall between them.

Afloat in that languid place between sleep and wakefulness, she let her eyelids slide closed again while a naughty picture of his body slid through her mind. *Jesse.* The name suited him. Tough yet tender. He'd welcomed her into his room. He'd put his arms around her in the parking lot, protected her from the storm.

Such a man would be an incredible lover. Anna couldn't say how she knew this. But she'd felt it, a galvanized shiver of awareness, while she stood in the sheltering circle of his arms with the snow blowing all around them. Awareness of his strength, and of the vague vulnerability that contradicted it. She'd been wrong to think him an impervious rock. Now that she knew his features, she read the unnamed history in the lines around his crystalline eyes—laughter. And the shadows beneath those eyes—grief. He'd been happy once. What had stolen that from him and brought him to this solitary place on Christmas Eve?

Unexpected desire surged low in her belly, burning her everywhere, pulsing heat between her thighs, making her painfully aware yet again of how long it had been since she'd known the touch, taste, scent of a man.

This one, with his paradox of darkness and light, mesmerized her. And being just a little afraid of him seemed to feed that fascination. She wanted to unlock his armor, see what dwelled beneath.

What if, for once, she took the road less traveled and followed the whisper of recklessness in her mind, the one that echoed the hot fantasies she'd entertained since first seeing him in the convenience store? What would he do if she threw all caution to the wind and met him at the bathroom door?

Merry Christmas, she'd say. May I unwrap you?

Before the scenario could play to fruition in her overheated mind, the door squeaked open and steam billowed out of the bathroom, followed by the delicious scent of soap and shampoo. Jesse appeared, his lean hips enfolded in a towel, his naked back turned to her as he retrieved the knapsack he'd placed by the sink.

She sat as still as a deer and watched the liquid play of sinew under his golden skin, her throat dry, her pulse pounding.

Rivulets of water trickled over the ridges and dips of his musculature, rushing to meet at the low dip of his back.

When he lifted his head, she froze.

The clean-shaven, sharply chiseled face reflected in the mirror belonged to someone new. But those eyes . . . deep, bright, exquisitely blue . . . they were the same. Filled with buried sadness, but under that, something more. Man's awareness of Woman. He knew she appraised him, measured him, contemplated the possibilities, and she didn't deny it by looking away.

They stared at each other in the mirror for much too long before Anna finally found her voice. "You shaved off your beard and mustache."

His mouth quirked and he rubbed a hand across his chin. "It's been a while. I feel kind of naked."

"You look different."

"You don't like the change?"

Her cheeks warmed as she tucked away the memory of her earlier fantasy. "Believe me, a part of me definitely liked the beard. But you're quite handsome this way. I like your face."

"Thank you," he said, his eyes finding hers again. Searching for his own answers.

Holy cow, she wanted him. And what, truly, did she have to lose, alone on Christmas night for the thirtieth time in her singular life?

One . . . two . . . three . . . jump. "So what are you thinking, Jesse, when you look at me like that?"

"Wondering what you're thinking when you're looking at *me* like that," he volleyed.

She had to smile, even though her heart threatened to hammer its way through her rib cage. "That's funny."

"Maybe a little."

Try, try again. "Well? Do you like what you see when you look at me?"

"Yes," he said, without preamble. Not that she gave him any choice.

Her brows lowered. "You're nice to say that, but I kind of put you on the spot just now."

"Maybe a little," he repeated.

Anna bit her lip. "Well. I like *you*, Jesse."

His strong throat moved when he swallowed. "That's good, seeing as how we're stuck here together."

An arid comment, but not a rejection.

She eased forward on the chair, her heart pounding. "I want to know you." The truth quavered just a little. Playtime was over.

He let the shaving lotion slide back into his knapsack, the muscles of his back flexing as he straightened. "Why?"

"I don't know. I'm drawn to you. Not just physically." When he didn't respond right away, she snapped out of her pleasurable haze and closed her eyes, humiliation chilling away the desire that had turned her insides to warm, sweet liquid. "Jeez . . . what am I doing?"

"I'm not sure." He braced his hands on the counter, all clean and sexy, watching her in the mirror with those blue, blue eyes. "Keep talking and maybe we'll figure it out together."

Not a rejection at all.

Just like that, the fire returned, rushed through her, simmering low in her belly. She licked her lips and straightened on the chair, the blanket sliding from her lap onto the floor. "I felt like this when I first saw you at the gas station, you know."

"Like how?" he prompted, his voice gone husky.

"Like . . . all squirrelly and . . . and hot." Her fingers dug into her thighs through the short velvet dress, braced for his rebuff, prepared for something far more frightening—his reciprocation. "You scare me to death. I haven't been with a man in a year, and even before that, I've only had a couple of boyfriends. I'm a long-termer when it comes to relationships. This isn't like me. I don't pick up strangers. You're a stranger."

"That's right." He turned at last to face her, but instead of approaching, he leaned his backside against the counter and let his sultry gaze slide down to her feet and back. "You want to change that?"

She tried to clear her throat, but all that came out was a squeak. Her body was aching and inflamed as though he'd touched her inside and out with his strong hands, yet all he'd done was make a few noncommittal comments, look at her with those watchful bedroom eyes, standing there unabashed in all his half-naked beauty . . .

Anything could happen next.

"Anna," he straightened away from the counter, the word playing on his lips as though he'd sampled it and liked what he tasted. "That's your name?"

"That's right," she said hoarsely.

"Anna," he said. "Come here."

4

When she didn't move right away, Jesse held out his hand, his heart lunging in his chest. Jesus, she looked vulnerable. She was small, so fragile in the face of an incredibly gutsy move.

Her proposition had sideswiped him. He couldn't have guessed she wanted him . . . didn't know why she did, when he had so little left to offer. Maybe it had something to do with being so lonely it hurt. He knew the feeling and he didn't want to hurt her. He didn't want to be hurt. Maybe if he touched her, cradled those soft, yielding curves against him and got the craving out of the way, he could end anything else that would expose him for the brittle shell he'd become.

Or maybe he was dreaming this entire scenario.

His hand started to drop, but then she rose from the chair

and crossed the six feet between them to take it. Her cool fingers laced through his, and she pressed against him, her free arm encircling his naked waist. Instantly his cock surged from half-mast to full hardness, too responsive to the slightest stimulation after so long. If she noticed, she didn't say anything. She could have been coy, suggestive, doused the heat between them with some crass comment that would shine a spotlight on what this truly was—a meaningless one-night stand.

Instead, she rubbed her nose against his bare chest like a languid cat, her lips finding the hollow at the base of his throat.

"Christ," he whispered, his head listing as she placed small, tentative kisses along the side of his neck. The scent of soap and fresh shampoo filled his senses. She'd showered, left off the stockings. Her shapely legs were golden and bare.

Between them his erection pushed against the towel, against her belly, answering any questions left unvoiced and demanding much more.

Still he spoke, one last grasp at sanity. "Why are you doing this?"

"Because all we have in this world right now is each other." She pulled back to look at him, her lashes heavy, her lips parted in invitation. "Because tonight I think you're as lost as I am. And because I think you're beautiful. You're so beautiful, Jesse."

He wrapped a hand in the tousled damp mane that tumbled to her shoulders. "And so you want me to fuck you." A test.

Anna didn't flinch. "I want you to touch me. To make love with me."

"I don't know what that is anymore," he whispered, and

rested his jaw against her temple where her pulse thudded a staccato rhythm. *She really is scared.* He was, too. His own heartbeat echoed hers, pounding in his throat, his chest, his engorged cock.

"It doesn't matter." Her words quavered as she caught his wrists and brought his hands up to cup her breasts. "Don't you have a wife? A girlfriend?"

"There's no one. Not in a year." He stared down at his fingers curving around the soft mounds of her breasts. Even through the velvet bodice of her dress and some stiff undergarment beneath it, her nipples poked his palms, tight little knots of arousal. He wanted to grasp the neckline and pull, tear it away from her slim body, suck and bite and lick every inch of her. She was petite; he could handle her, twist and turn and move her where he wanted her, how he wanted her, which was in every possible way. Now. *Right now.*

When Anna's gentle fingers cupped the back of his neck, the ferocity in him stilled.

Make love to me, she'd said. By God, he would remember how. She would show him.

Grasping her waist, Jesse turned her and lifted her onto the counter by the sink, putting them at eye level. She had big liquid eyes, a tender mouth that invited a sliding tongue. Pacing himself, he ducked his head, caught her lips gently, feathered his mouth across hers, once, twice, nudging his way inside with soft, non-threatening kisses, a softer probe with the tip of his tongue. Licking, flicking, meeting her tongue and darting away again, he savored the faint whiskey taste of her until her fingers dug into his back and her breathing fractured into small explosions.

It was all the encouragement he needed. His fingers slid beneath her dress and up one bare thigh to the incredible heat and dampness of her sex, where he paused, and stroked, and teased until her pelvis lifted from the counter in search of a firmer touch. Her panties were in the way, but he played her through them, driving them both higher with each stroke of his thumb, to a place where they couldn't turn back.

Groaning her frustration, Anna sought to kiss his mouth again, but Jesse was intent. He dragged her hips closer to the edge of the counter, pinning her hands to the Formica surface, and dropped to his knees before her.

"No . . ." It was half-plea, half-protest, when he grasped her legs to edge them apart and his intention became clear.

"No?" He looked up at her flushed face, at the way her hair tumbled, sleep-sexy, around her cheeks. "No, you don't want me to strip you naked and eat you until you come?"

"I don't know. I haven't . . . I don't . . ." Her eyelids fluttered open, her hand slipping from his grasp and finding its way into his hair. God, he liked the way she touched him. He wanted to feel those gentle fingers tangled and tugging for dear life while she screamed her pleasure beneath his mouth. He wanted to drive his tongue deep into her wetness and swallow her whole.

"Spread your legs for me, Anna," he whispered, and when she did, just a little, he caught the sole of her foot against his bare chest to hold her there, open to him, vulnerable.

The sultry, aroused scent of her perfume and raw desire filled his senses as he nuzzled his way up the inside of her thigh, nipping, licking through the thin barrier of her panties.

The soft material was silken with her body's need as though she'd been aroused for some time.

"God, you're so wet."

Instantly her legs pressed closed. "I know, I know. Just looking at you in the convenience store made me that way." She squeezed her eyes closed at her own confession, two spots of crimson appearing high on her cheeks, but Jesse smiled and pressed a kiss of reverence against her knee.

"Anna, don't do that. You know how long I've been hard? Maybe since you stepped foot into my motel room. Why do you think I got in the shower while you were asleep?"

"I don't know . . ."

He studied her fluttering lashes. "To jack off like some kind of desperate fool."

Her eyelids flew open and she stared down into his face, a shudder moving through her. "Did you?"

"In the end, no." He nuzzled her other knee. "Maybe some part of me was hoping you'd let me do this instead."

"Good," came the husky response, and she shifted her knees apart as though he'd uttered "Open Sesame."

"Lean back against the mirror and lift up a little." When she obliged, he drew the bikinis down to her ankles. They dangled, uselessly frilly and forgotten, from one bare foot, while he stroked the outside of her naked hips beneath the dress. Then shifting to his haunches, he pushed the hem of her dress up her shapely thighs, up, up, exposing every creamy inch of her skin, and when her neatly shaven mound came into view, he closed his eyes and gripped the counter's edge on either side of her to squelch the rush of desire that threatened to undo him.

It would be so easy to stand up, grasp her hips and pull her forward to meet his relentless thrust. To push inside her, deep, deeper, then back again, dragging through all that silky wetness, back and forth in measured lunges, setting fire to her senses, and to his own. But her request—her challenge—so brave, so shaky, echoed in his overheated mind. *Make love to me.*

And so, parting her slick folds with his thumbs, he leaned forward and with the tip of his tongue found the swollen bead of her clitoris.

"Oh!" Her entire body jerked, and his own muscles clenched in response, perspiration dampening his limbs.

He wanted to come, right then and there.

He shifted, regrouped, breathed in the clean, sexy scent of her skin and, beneath that, the perfume of her desire. Pacing himself. Reveling, for the first time in a million forevers, in beauty and pleasure. And when he was ready, he leaned forward again and let his tongue explore her, made lazy circles around and around the tiny nub at the top of her sex until she was trembling. While his fingers held her open to him, his tongue glided lower, through the moisture that slicked her flesh, savoring her salty-sweet flavor as he recalled from some sleeping part of him what made a woman sing, what made her sigh, what made her scream with pleasure.

Maybe Jesse didn't know Anna, but he'd guessed just right.

When he spread her wider with his fingertips and unexpectedly plunged his tongue into her core, she uttered a choked cry and her hands clutched his shoulders, his neck, his hair, blindly seeking to anchor herself under his tender assault. "Oh God, Oh God, Oh *God!*" Thrashing shudders lifted her pelvis and rocked her against his mouth as she climaxed under his tongue.

Still Jesse lapped and licked her, probing, stroking, until she collapsed against the mirror and her fingers loosened their death grip on his hair. Then he grasped the edge of the counter and rose on legs that quaked.

When her lashes lifted and her somnolent brown gaze locked with his, she didn't speak. No words were necessary. He helped her off the counter and drew her toward the bed a few feet away, where she sat on the edge, considering him, his naked torso, the blatant tent his erection made beneath the snug towel as he stood in front of her.

The orgasm he'd given her had apparently stripped away her inhibitions and now she sat before him, tousled, lush, vibrating with sensuous intent. This night could go so very wrong.

Or so very right.

Lost, he squeezed his eyes closed and gave himself over to her. *Make love to me, too, Anna. Make me forget everything but pleasure.*

And she did. Jesse vaguely registered the rush of cool air on his skin as she unknotted his towel and drew it away from his body, the murmur of approval she uttered as she took in the sight of his need, then her hands were clutching his naked ass and her hot, sweet mouth engulfed his cock, sucking it deep into scalding wetness.

Trembling, he let his hands find her hair and buried them in silky thick luxury. He wanted to rub those satin strands over his erection, rub and rub until he came in hard, pulsing shudders. He wanted to thrust deep into her mouth, again, again, feel the compression of her throat around him as she swallowed everything he had to give. His agony. His need. His pleasure.

There was so much he wanted, and so little time. Forcing his eyes open, he stared down at her and watched the smooth ride of his shaft pushing between her lips, then its reappearance, red-hot, impossibly harder and wet from the insistent stroke of her tongue. Despite her innate innocence, she was damned good at this. Her hands gripped his hips and guided him between her lips again, her thumbs caressing the sensitive spots inside his hipbones. Sucking him in as deep as he would go. Pulling back and playing the head of his penis with her firm, dancing tongue before taking him again in strong, hungry pulls.

"I'm going to come," he panted.

She drew back and met his eyes. "Not yet." The world tilted as she unexpectedly pulled him down with her, and he caught himself before he crushed her beneath him on the mattress. And then her thighs were riding his hips and he was moving against her, driving his hard penis against her slippery chasm, and there was so much wetness . . . from her, from him, the scent of heat and want an earthy ambrosia between them.

Jesse was frantic. Before he could stop himself, before he could think, he shoved her dress around her waist, grasped his shaft with the other and found her quivering, wet entrance with the driving tip of his cock.

"Come inside me," she breathed against his ear, giving him the permission he needed.

He thrust firm and deep within her, to the hilt. No protection in any form, not even on his heart.

"*Ah* . . ." An indecipherable sound tore from the center of his chest. A sound of agony. A sound of joy.

He was raw. "Oh God."

"It's okay, Jess, it's fine . . ." Breathing mindless encouragement, Anna pulled her knees up high to cradle his hips and took him even deeper, her hair spilled wildly beneath her, her fingers grasping at his back, his ribs, his undulating backside, then at last the crumpled bedspread, taking it with her as his fierce rhythmic thrusts drove and drove and drove her up the mattress.

"Christ, you feel . . . so . . . *good*." He moved spasmodically, like a machine beyond his own control. This was more than fucking. The way she scalded him, enclosed him, down to the very heart of him . . . he'd never felt sensation so intense.

Release built to unbearable heights in Jesse's cock, filled it to bursting, and he tried to slow, to delay the explosion, but she was whispering hot words against his ear—"*Oh yes, oh please yes*—" thrusting back almost faster than he could plunge inside her, and then she climaxed again, her cries lost beneath the roar in his ears, and it was too late. He heard himself from a distance, groaning desperate words from a primal, universal language, months of pain and emptiness jetting inside her as he came with an intensity that detonated stars before his eyes.

It went on and on, spasms of ecstasy clenching and draining, painful and incredible and cleansing. When the stars faded, his head sagged against her shoulder, and for a moment he allowed himself to be held in warmth and what felt strangely—impossibly—like love.

"Jesse," she whispered against his cheek, and scattered light, soothing kisses over his damp shoulder. "Jess."

For an instant he lolled in the loveliness of Anna, her peace, her tenderness. Trying to remember what was wrong in his life that had brought him, ironically, to this place of joy. Because he'd forgotten. For just a second, he'd forgotten.

And then he remembered. The grief returned with a vengeance, threatening what little dignity he'd brought to this naked place. Easing off her, he rolled to his back and flung an arm over his eyes, struggling to breathe, to force the emotions back into the bottomless well he'd long feared would one day be unlocked.

He hadn't dreamed a stranger might hold the key.

He didn't know her. Hadn't wanted to. Hadn't meant for this day to become so lost and misguided, and God, where was his path to self-destruction leading him this time? The knot in his throat had nothing to do with the anger and pain that had sustained him up until now. This woman had exposed his scars with one look. *Jesus.* One touch. A little sympathy from a stranger, and he wanted to weep like some kind of idiot kid.

Quiet, Anna shifted onto her side to face him. He sensed the touch of her luminous gaze on every part of him, as though she could read the darkness etched on his heart. Her brown eyes were too probing, too aware. It was the first thing he'd noticed about her, standing beside him at the gas station coffee counter. Her velvety brown eyes, her silken soul.

"Jesse?"

When she reached out and moved his arm away from his face, he grasped her wrist to push her back . . . and failed as he registered the soft resilience of her skin, the warm, musky fragrance of a woman's desire that rose from beneath the crumpled dress. His fingers gentled to caress her, to measure the fine breadth of her wrist as he brought it to his lips and kissed the tender flesh where her pulse hammered erratically.

"You're so damned beautiful," he murmured, and that was all, because his gratitude choked anything more. She said nothing, just laid her head on her crooked elbow, watching him revel in her.

He'd wanted to touch her like this since he'd first seen her. To know the surface of her body, and beyond that, her heart. To learn the lush resilience of her mouth, the flicker of her tongue, the heat of her kiss, breathing life back into him.

A fleeting fantasy . . . yet here they were. The impossible could still happen after all.

Jesse Proffitt could still feel something besides pain.

"Can I ask you a question?" Anna finally spoke, her voice hushed, as though the room were a sacred place. Maybe it was, she thought. They'd christened it thus.

"What is it?" He rolled to his side to meet her, and they lay nose-to-nose, elbows bent beneath their heads.

"Why aren't you married?"

It was none of her business, but she wanted something more of him to take with her when they parted. Something more than the incredible pleasure he'd given her, that they'd given each other.

He swallowed and reached out to move a wayward strand of

hair from her cheek. "I used to be married. We were together eleven years. We divorced last year."

"Oh." Her gaze slid away as she assimilated the information and tried to conjure a scenario. What kind of woman had he loved enough to marry? Was she funny? Bright? Beautiful? Did she know how to touch him just right? Could he make her go all wet and weak with one look from those incredible blue eyes of his? And a really masochistic part of Anna wondered, how many times had this woman taken him inside her body and heard those magic words of desire and need whispered against her hair?

You feel so good . . . you're so damned beautiful . . .

"Did you leave her?" she asked, and winced at the sound of her own driving inquisitiveness.

"Well . . ." He rolled to his back and exhaled, one hand absently rubbing his stomach as he thought about his answer. "I guess that depends on which one of us you ask. On paper, she left me. She had justifiable reasons. I guess I drove her away. I don't know." He sighed again, his profile limned by the frail glow from the lamp. "We were happy for a while, at first. She was a real estate agent. I was a writer. We had money, a nice house. And then we had a child. A son."

Anna hesitated, sensing the shift of currents in the night. Languid arousal had slid into something dark and raw. "Where is your son now?"

"He died eighteen months ago." It was a flat statement, an offering of emotionless facts, and yet the grief behind it stole the breath from her lungs.

It explained so much, all of a sudden. This was a key to who

Jesse was. And she couldn't help herself when she asked softly, "What happened to him?"

For a long time Jesse didn't answer, and Anna's cheeks warmed with each excruciating second that passed in silence. She'd crossed the invisible barrier he wore around himself like armor. Her prying had shattered all the delicious, languid intimacy between them.

Then his husky words rent the quiet. "He was hit by a drunk driver on the street in front of our house."

Anna swallowed, trying to read his features in the shadows. It was impossible. But his words bled an anguish she couldn't begin to measure.

"He was six years old."

"Oh, Jesse . . ." she scooted closer to him, her palm finding his cheek in the shadows. "I have no right to pry like this, but . . . if you want to tell me, I'll listen."

"I don't know. I haven't . . . I don't know."

"It's okay." She quickly accepted his shaken reply, moved by it into acquiescence and shame. "I'm so sorry. I shouldn't have asked."

The sheets rustled as he shifted to look at her. "Shouldn't you? Look at us, Anna. Two complete strangers. Yet I feel like I've been closer to you tonight than maybe anyone, ever. If there's anyone who I want to spill my poison with, it's you."

"Then talk to me." She cupped his face in one hand, the other tracing the somber line of his mouth. He had beautiful, sculpted lips for a man. He had a truth to tell, *poison,* as he'd called it, so potent that he carried it with him like his own secret potion. She could see the toxic anguish in his eyes, which flashed like polished stone in the gloom.

His words burst out, choked and laughing at the same time. "I thought that losing a child happened to other people. He was there every day, a part of my life, a part of me, more than my own breath. Can you imagine losing an arm or leg? How about both arms? Both legs? You can't even compare that agony to what it felt like losing Daniel."

Anna swallowed the useless words of consolation welling on her lips. Something told her that her silence was far more valuable now as he purged his truth.

"It was spring, beautiful, warm. He asked me if he could play in the yard with the other kids. Did you finish your homework, I said. Like that's even important for a kid who's just turned six." Jesse was weeping now, a flood of anguish that she met and embraced with silent strength. "He hadn't finished his homework, he needed help on the math, but I needed to write—I had an opinion column in a local paper, and if you asked me now what my oh-so-fucking-important opinion was that day, I couldn't tell you." Wiping his eyes, he uttered a short, self-effacing laugh. "I had a long way to fall to be humbled, and trust me, I'm there now. But that day—I wanted peace and quiet. I told him to go outside. And when he got there, his buddies from next door were out playing football, except their damn dog kept stealing the ball. They told me later Daniel was the only one to give chase when the dog darted out into the road. And—" He stopped, too choked, and for a moment there was only silence, while his torn breathing shattered the night, and Anna's cheeks grew wet with tears of sympathy.

"And see, there was this homeless guy, an alcoholic, who had holed up temporarily with his brother a couple of streets over. He had a few drunk driving citations under his belt, but his lawyer brother kept digging him out, and digging him out. Doing him a favor, he thought. That's what brothers do for each other. While Daniel was playing with his friends, this guy got drunk, borrowed his brother's new sports car and took it for an afternoon joyride. Down the street. Down the next street. Then down our street, going fifty miles an hour. And he didn't even remember hitting my son, later, when they caught him. He was so drunk, he didn't remember killing a child. My child."

"I'm so sorry," Anna whispered, leaning to kiss the corner of his mouth. "So, so sorry."

"Daniel was only six." Jesse's hand covered Anna's to hold it against his hot, tear-streaked face. "Six years old when he died, and I died with him. Every time I say the words aloud, I die again."

She stroked his cheek, blind in the dark, blind to who he was, only that he was Jesse, a stranger full of secrets, and perhaps he'd shared with her the biggest one.

She could share with him, too. Her sympathy. Her touch. Herself. "Jesse," she whispered, and lifting her head, she found his trembling mouth with her kiss.

So much time had passed since he'd known pleasure of any kind, much less this potent, sweet arousal flaring between them again. He tried to feel guilty for letting it dilute his grief, but desire rushed through him anew, tensing every muscle as he slid his hand up her arm and roughly pushed the dress off her shoulder. *So smooth, her skin. Like satin.*

Hot with shame, with too many tears, he started to apologize for his outburst, but she leaned closer to capture his mouth more fully, swallowing his agony, one hand stroking his hair, the other gliding over his chest to caress his stomach, to trace around his navel, then down his flank, and when he thought he'd go crazy for want of her, to firmly grasp his aching erection.

The electric contact of her fingers on his cock nearly sent him through the roof. *"Anna . . ."*

"Make love to me again," she whispered, and grasping his hands, guided them to her small, firm breasts through the lacy brassiere she still wore.

He couldn't think, couldn't rationalize, *couldn't stop.* Her dress was caught around her waist, the zipper buried beneath the drooping bodice. His shaking fingers didn't work well enough to find it, so he sat up, grasped the back of the bodice and pulled.

Anna didn't flinch at the telltale ripping sound. Scrambling to her knees beside him, she reached behind her, freed herself from the strapless bra and drew the unsalvageable dress up and over her head. The dress rustled to a forlorn heap on the floor.

Flushed, ruffled, and goddess-beautiful to his aching eyes, she met his gaze squarely and said, "Again. Please. Now."

"Ride me," he ordered, half mindless as he braced his back against the cold headboard and led her to sit astride him.

She found his shaft with a confident hand, rubbed herself against the engorged head, teasing, beckoning, and then slowly sank down on him in measured increments until they both gasped with the ecstasy of it. For a moment neither moved, then Jesse's attention shifted from her rapt features to her naked breasts, and he cupped them for the first time, gently, in reverence, filling his palms with their weight, thumbing the small nipples into turgid points.

How could he have taken her the first time without touching every part of her first? Without poring over her, learning each curve, each point of delight? She was perfect, the most desirable woman he'd ever known, and for tonight, no one and nothing else existed but them in this tiny, enchanted room.

Everything slowed then, as the anguish seeped away like swirling blood washed down a drain. He leaned forward and caught her nipple between his lips, flicked it with his tongue. Tugged a little until she shivered and arched her back. He scissored his teeth gently across it and felt the heavy, quick-ened drum of her pulse in response, the tiny contractions of her silken muscles around his shaft with each tug, as though an invisible string stretched between her nipple and her womb.

Anna watched him in the spellbound silence, her long brown hair fallen around them, the only sound between them the harsh seesaw of their breathing. When he lifted his head in a silent request for her kiss, she feathered her lips across his open, panting mouth. Then she rose and fell once, twice, riding his cock with a measured deliberateness that dumped every sane, human thought from his mind and sent an orgasm rushing up his shaft like fire.

"Please," he gritted. "Not yet."

"Yes," she whispered fiercely. "Now." And she cradled his head against her breasts, a strangely protective gesture that granted Jesse permission to take his pleasure without inhibition.

Biting back the wild sounds rising in his chest, he gripped her hips, pushed high and hard and exploded, every shudder of his body in rhythmic correlation to the pulsing jets he shot inside her.

And while he was still shuddering, he grasped her waist and ground her against the rigid root of his cock, all his attention focused on her pleasured face, the way she clutched his shoulders and rode him frantically in return.

There was nothing more beautiful to Jesse than the sight of her like this. *Anna.* He would remember her forever.

She cried his name when she came, her head thrown back, graceful throat flexing with the attempt to swallow the feral sounds of ecstasy. She bathed him in her essence and her peace, and drew the darkness from him.

In the aftermath, they slid down and apart and finally beneath the sheets, only to flow back together again, limbs entangled as they shared a pillow.

When Jesse could talk, he said, "Anna, Anna, Anna." A surrendering sigh. A lover's accolade.

She smiled and rubbed her lips against his still pounding heart.

"I ruined your dress," he said after another minute of floating in the healing quiet.

"Damn you," she murmured aridly.

He lifted his head to meet her sleepy cocoa eyes, noting the way she held him, with arms and legs surrounding him but not clinging, as though to say, *You can run if you need to.*

What he wanted—needed—was to stay.

"You can wear my flannel shirt and a pair of jeans I brought with me," he went on, fingering a silky strand of her hair where it lay against the pillow.

"I'll be the hit of the party, if I ever make it there." Anna stretched and smiled at him, languid and blissfully mindless of her rumpled state. He liked that about her, that lack of self-consciousness. She was innately sensuous, too. An incredible lover, and no doubt she'd show him, slower and easier, if he could get past wanting to fuck her into tomorrow. If he could stop himself from spurting the minute she touched him.

He'd just have to practice with her until he got it right.

5

In the soft blue morning light that pierced the gap in the curtains, they dressed without speaking. After showering together to bathe away the night's desire and merely eliciting more, both were too drowsy for anything beyond long glances and tender smiles. Jesse chuckled at the sight of Anna's lithe hips swimming in his jeans. She had rolled the cuffs several times and didn't seem one bit awkward in the oversized flannel shirt he'd given her. The now-shabby velvet pumps were an interesting touch, too. Star-struck, he watched her wiggle into them with a helpless smile.

When they were packed, he dragged his knapsack and helmet off the table and stopped her before she could open the door.

"Merry Christmas, baby," he whispered, nuzzling her tousled hair.

"Merry Christmas." Her arms crept around his waist, and they stood there for a moment, each wondering if the night's storm—inside their hearts and outside in the world—had passed.

Anna turned her head to look at him as she opened the door, wondering what to say to ease the sudden unease, but Jesse was staring past her, squinting into the morning sun.

She whipped around.

The world was green and clear, the birds chirping beneath a cornflower sky.

Not a sign of white powder to be found.

Stepping out into the parking lot, she made a slow circle, her incredulous eyes taking in the utterly impossible.

Where was all the snow?

Jesse followed her, his steps slow as he looked around. "I can't believe what I'm seeing."

"There was a storm, though," Anna began, her voice trembling. "You saw it too—the drifts, the ice—there's no way it could have melted this quickly . . ."

"There was a storm," he echoed, and they lapsed into silence, staring at each other in disbelief.

Then Jesse shouldered his backpack and tucked his helmet beneath his arm. "Let's check out of the motel," he told her. "We'll ask the clerk what he saw last night."

Inside the tiny lobby, everything was the same as Anna had remembered it, except the jolly bearded guy in the suspenders was gone, replaced by a chunky teenager with ear piercings *ad nauseum* and a gleaming set of braces on her smiling, gum-snapping teeth.

"Merry Christmas," she said cheerfully. "Did y'all enjoy your stay?"

Jesse cast Anna a meaningful glance. "Absolutely."

"It was wonderful," she added, and for a second she forgot the missing snow, the broken-down Toyota, the wrecked motorcycle, the magnificent strangeness of it all. Only Jesse was there, Jesse with his blue eyes and gentle, skillful hands. A man full of shadow and light, and a fathomless grief he held close to his soul. Maybe they'd part ways forever today, but no matter what she failed to learn about him in their few remaining moments, he was no longer a stranger to her heart.

". . . And we're just curious," he was telling the clerk, his lean cheeks flushing. "Did it snow around here last night?"

The teenager laughed. "Heck, no. It's been in the seventies all week. It's enough to kill the Christmas spirit, know what I mean?"

Anna stilled. Beneath the counter, Jesse's hand closed around hers and gently squeezed.

"Well, that's funny." She recovered, keeping her voice steady when what she really wanted was to reach across the counter and shake the girl. "The old guy who checked us in last night said something about snow."

The girl leaned her elbow by the register. "What old guy? You mean here? We don't have any men working here. Martha was on duty last night."

A huff of disbelief burst from Anna's chest. "Look, we're not idiots. There *was* an old guy here behind the counter. He was bald, had a white beard and he was dressed funny, with stripes and suspenders, kind of elfish—"

"I reckon it was Santa Claus," the girl said with a laughing snort. "Serious now, only Martha was here, unless she's seein' some guy, and she'd tell me because she pretty much hates men in general, 'specially the ones 'round here, so I sure don't think that's it."

"That's it!" Anna snapped her fingers, her eyes widening.

"How do you know?" the clerk frowned at her. "Martha's a friend of my mama's, and I can tell you if she was datin' some old guy, I would surely hear about—"

"No. I mean, what you said before—about the man who was here. He did look—and act—exactly like—" Anna glanced at Jesse in a mixture of abject embarrassment and wonder. "I-I think it was . . . Santa. And this place really must be . . ." her breath left her chest on a strangled note. "*The Holiday Inn.*"

"Lady, you're turned around." The girl waved her hand, as though the conversation was perfectly viable. "This here's the Magnolia Motel. The Holiday Inn's down two exits and beyond the overpass. It's the big conference center. You can't miss it."

"But the sign out there says—"

"Magnolia Motel." Jesse's low voice broke through Anna's fog of agitation as he gazed out the window. "The sign's right there."

She stared in the direction where he pointed and shook her head. "What the hell happened here last night?"

"Maybe a little too much celebrating, if you ask me," the girl muttered.

"A visit from St. Nick," Anna whispered, meeting Jesse's eyes. "The best gift ever. Wouldn't you agree?"

"I would definitely agree." He let the curtain fall and moved toward her, both of them forgetting the invasive presence of the gawking teenaged desk clerk. When he bent his head to kiss Anna, he quietly laid the room key on the desk and slid it toward the girl.

Swiping it off the countertop, she backed away from the two crazy people in her lobby. "All righty, then. Thanks for staying at the Magnolia Motel. Y'all have a nice day." And she fled into the office.

Neither Jesse nor Anna said a word when they found the Toyota parked in an inconspicuous spot outside the motel lobby, and a few feet beyond it, Jesse's motorcycle, unscathed.

They stood between the two vehicles for a while, bewildered, maybe a little scared.

Jesse was the first to laugh. He laughed and laughed, and after a moment an answering smile crept across Anna's face. There was no explanation for the last twenty-four hours, beyond two lost souls finding each other through an impossible storm. Finding comfort. Finding love's sweet potential. What more could one want for Christmas?

"Anna, what's your last name?" He caught her hand and pulled her, grinning helplessly, against him.

"Shea," she said.

"I'm Jesse Proffitt."

"Nice to meet you," she said, her smile widening.

"Anna Shea, do you believe in magic?"

"After last night, do you even need to ask?" She stood on tiptoe and slid her arms around his neck. "Don't you?"

"I didn't for so long." His humor faded as he gazed down

into her face. "Until you showed up in a magic storm, and brought me to this magic place, and touched me with your magic hands. You made me believe in magic and so much more. Thank you." He raised her hand to his lips and kissed her knuckles. Then, "I have another question for you."

"What is it?" she asked, tears and laughter shining in her eyes.

"Tell me, Anna Shea . . . what are you doing New Year's Eve?"

Epilogue

From his perch on a kitchen chair, eight-year-old Justin Proffitt watched his mom prepare dinner, his dark brows drawn down in troubled thought. After a moment he was ready with his yearly arsenal of questions.

"Okay, so how did you meet Dad again?"

She smiled as she withdrew a bag of vegetables from the refrigerator. "Santa Claus introduced us."

Justin wasn't so sure anymore that Santa really existed. Especially because he'd recently seen his dad wrestling a large box down to the basement that looked like the racecar track he'd requested in his yearly letter to the North Pole.

"Mom, that whole thing sounds made up."

"It's true. We got lost in a snowstorm on the highway. Dad was riding a motorcycle and I was driving a car. When he slid on the ice and fell off his bike, I pulled over to help him.

And soon we found out that there never was a snowstorm."

"So Santa made the snow so you guys would meet."

"Right."

He scowled, but before he could pin her down for more details, his father came downstairs from his office and stopped to kiss Justin on the head.

"How are you, kiddo? Enjoying your first day of winter break?"

"It's okay, I guess." Which meant, *I'm bored.* They hadn't seen each other all morning. Justin wasn't supposed to interrupt him while he was writing, and today had been especially difficult. Justin had awakened to a world blanketed in fluffy whiteness, which meant sledding, snowball fights, and snowman build-offs with the neighborhood kids, and no team could build as fat and tall a snowman as Justin and his dad. But today Jesse had a "deadline," which meant little to Justin except the nothing-to-dos.

The two younger boys who lived across the street laughed and made fun of the crappy snowman he'd tried to build alone. Since he wasn't allowed to leave the yard, he couldn't go across the street and punch them out the way they deserved. So he'd come in, defeated, and pulled out his art supplies to color at the kitchen table.

"Dad." He turned to watch him as Jesse set a hand on his wife's pregnant belly and leaned around her to steal a carrot from the pile of vegetables she was chopping. "Are you guys Santa Claus?"

Jesse turned to regard him with a faint smile. "Haven't we had this discussion? Like fifty times since October?"

"I guess." Justin sighed. "It's just that most of my friends' parents don't believe in him. You guys are the only ones who still act like he's real. And you don't just believe in him. You have this whole story about how he helped you meet each other." He looked down. "It's kind of embarrassing, so don't tell anyone else, okay? Nobody has to know."

"The only person we've told that story to is you," Jesse said, crossing the kitchen to sit at the table beside him. "You're the only one whose opinion matters to us. And if you don't believe in Santa Claus anymore, that's your business. But the story stays the same. We know how we met. Santa set us up."

Justin stared hard at him, waiting for him to crack a smile, but his dad just gazed back without blinking.

His mom set down the chopping knife and crossed to the refrigerator again. "We've never lied to you about anything else, have we?"

He thought for a moment, then shrugged. "I guess not." Which was good, because really he wanted to believe in Santa, even though his friends had stopped. They sure would be sorry one day if it turned out his parents were right.

"Hey, Dad." Justin poked at Jesse's hand with an unused paintbrush. "Can me and you go out in the snow for a while?"

"You and I."

"That's what I said."

"I thought you'd never ask."

"But what about your deadline?"

Jesse looked skyward and scratched his chin. "Deadline? What deadline? Last one out has to wash the dishes after dinner." Before Justin could react, his dad bolted from the chair. Justin raced after him, swerved in front of him and tried to block the entrance to the foyer, but Jesse lifted and threw him, shouting with laughter, over his shoulder like a sack of flour. "Anna, get out the lotion—Justy's going to have dishpan hands tonight!"

Father and son made a noisy exit down the stairs, leaving Anna smiling to herself in the kitchen. She turned and with a heart full of joy, watched her boys through the window over the sink.

Her beautiful, happy boys.

Once Jesse believed he would never know the love of a child again, the sound of his own boy's laughter, the way a father felt when his son walked tall in his wake. Now he had it all in spades, because he was as much Justin's world as Justin was his. And the best part was that Jesse hadn't been afraid to love again when his second son was placed in his arms, or to remember—and cherish—the sweet, lost boy of his shattered past.

How far Jesse and Anna had come together. She'd never thought she wanted children until she met him. He made her believe anything was not only possible, but well deserved. He was her rock, upon which she'd built a life of happiness. And she was his. A risky prospect, placing one's heart in the hands of such an infallible creature as another human being. Such was love—sometimes frightening, sometimes perilous, and always, *always* magnificent.

She absently caressed her hard, rounded belly as she studied her family through the window. Only three more weeks, and then there would be four.

"Yes, Katie Proffitt," she assured her unborn little girl, the first of many times to come. "There really is a Santa Claus. Let me tell you how I know . . ."

His Christmas Cara

Shiloh Walker

To everybody . . . Merry Christmas, keep the spirit
of the season in your heart throughout the year.
My family . . . what do you want for Christmas . . .
I'll give you the moon if I can.

Eben Marley walked out of the main offices of Venture Advertising, his briefcase held loosely in one hand, his eyes flicking to his watch. The merry calls all around him went unheeded.

Merry Christmas!

Happy New Year!

Somebody brushed a hand down his arm, and a scent he had never forgotten surrounded him.

Slowly, he turned his head, already knowing who he'd see—Cara.

The pretty administrative assistant smiled at him, her eyes not reflecting the smile. A charming dimple winked in her cheek as she brushed her hair back out of her face.

The soft scent of her body drifted to his nostrils and he breathed it in deep, feeling it like a punch in his belly.

Three years . . . He could recall just how long it had been, and his body flared to sudden rampant life.

"Cara," he said, inclining his head at her, lifting a brow as he waited.

Maybe . . . just maybe . . . The thought never had time to complete itself. "I hope you have a Merry Christmas, Mr. Marley," she said before cutting sharply to the right to catch up with some friends.

Mr. Marley.

As she walked away, those words mocked him. A three-year-old memory loomed large in his mind. Just one night— one that had haunted every waking thought for months, until finally, he'd forced her out of his thoughts, suppressing the memory of that night. Except for his dreams.

She still haunted his dreams.

One night . . . that pretty admin, in the elevator at the Grand as he whisked her up to a room where he had fucked her throughout the night, starting with a quickie in the elevator after he'd pushed the stop button. It had ended with him leaving her the next morning with orders for his driver to take her home while he attended to business.

As she walked away, her head bent low against the wind, a memory of that sleek little body wrapped around his, grabbed him by the throat—err, maybe the throat wasn't a good term, he mused as his cock started to throb within the constraints of his underwear and trousers.

Now destined to spend the night hungering for another taste of her, he rolled his eyes and muttered, "Yeah . . . Merry Christmas."

His idea of "merry" was knowing how much money people sank into advertising for Christmas. His company's profits were above last year's, and his own personal bank account was all but groaning.

That was the only thing that interested him about Christmas. Sooner or later, he might slow down enough to have some fun. A rich, husky laugh reached his ears, drifting to him on the wind, as he arrived at the black car waiting at the curb. He stopped, turned his head—the admin assistant, laughing in delight as she accepted a gift from somebody Eben placed as being in accounting.

A night with her definitely would be an improvement over the paperwork he planned to go over. She was grinning with delight as she tore into the present, and he groaned as another image, one he hadn't thought of in years, rushed to the front of his mind . . . that girl . . . Cara . . . sliding him that wide, wicked grin just before she'd closed her lips over his cock.

Tearing his eyes away from her lovely face, he ducked through the car door, telling Jacob, "I want to stop by the bank on the way home."

"Sir, the banks closed at noon today—about thirty minutes ago," Jacob said, his face stiff, eyes blank.

"Closed? Why— Damn it. Never mind, Christmas," he muttered, scrubbing a hand over his face. "Take me on home then. Hell, I should have stayed and gotten more work done."

"Work late? On Christmas Eve?" Jacob said gently. "C'mon, boss. Have a little fun."

Have a little fun . . . Unwillingly, his eyes drifted back to

Cara as she threw her arms around the other woman's neck, obviously delighted with whatever gift she had received.

Shaking his head, he tore his mind away from her and laughed, running a hand through his tousled hair. "I make money for fun, Jacob. Let's get moving," he said, sitting back and opening his briefcase, pulling out a handful of files to flip through on the drive.

Cara Winston glanced over her shoulder as that blond head ducked inside his sleek, sexy Benz and felt her heart flutter. Well, he hadn't growled at her when she wished him a Merry Christmas. There had also been a look of recognition in his eyes, of heat.

Damn it, why in the hell couldn't she stop thinking about him?

Why didn't she hate him?

Hell, now that wasn't really fair. He had told her, right off the bat, I want sex, one night, that's all. What gave her the right to still be hurt over his quick and total dismissal the morning after that rather spectacular night together?

No right . . . at all, she reminded herself.

"Give it up, Cara," somebody advised.

Cara glanced back and saw Toni shaking her head. "He's a waste of time," Toni continued. "Hell, this is the first year in the ten I've been here that he finally gave up trying to get people to work on Christmas. And he didn't even want to pay overtime. I can't believe he actually gave us a half day off."

"Well, I had to take it without pay," Chloe said, rolling her eyes. "I didn't have any time left."

Somebody Cara didn't recognize snickered and said, "Total waste. I bet the only thing that turns him on is seeing profit and shareholder info, and gross revenue statements."

Cara shivered, her lids drooping. No, that wasn't true. Her nipples tightened as she recalled just exactly how turned on he could get, that raw, hungry look on his face, replacing that cool, blank exterior . . . No, not true at all.

Swallowing, she shook her head, shoving those memories away.

She had too much to do, and reminiscing over one wonderful night wasn't going to get it done. Sighing, she turned and hugged her friends. "I've got to go. Duty calls," she said, waggling her fingers at them before turning away and heading for the garage.

Jacob kept sliding him odd glances in the mirror.

At first, as he relived that night with Cara, he hadn't noticed.

But the sensation of being watched sank in, and he looked up with narrowed eyes to see Jacob studying him in the rearview mirror, instead of focusing on the drive as he normally did.

Eben tried pretty damned hard to ignore him. Jacob was the first decent driver he'd had in months, easily. Since he'd fired Tom, he thought. Of course, Tom had kept nagging him about a raise.

Subtly, but hell, he'd given the man a raise six months earlier. He was still driving the same damned distance, still did the same damn thing every day. Why in the hell give him another raise? Especially since he seemed obligated to give everybody at Venture a raise at Christmas.

Jacob had appeared from the agency Eben had contacted about two weeks ago. Silent, for the most part, and respectful, keeping his eyes averted and his questions to himself. Finally, somebody who understood that Eben wanted a driver, not a golf buddy, a drinking buddy, a fishing buddy . . . just a driver.

But those sidelong looks when the black man thought his boss wasn't looking, they were starting to piss Eben off.

He sighed, and flipped through a few more pages before glancing out the window. He scowled as he realized they were speeding down 64 West, toward Louisville, in the opposite direction of home. "So, Jacob . . . Have you forgotten where I live?" he asked casually, mentally tallying up a mark against Jacob. That's one. He gave his employees three chances when they fucked up. And three only.

"No, Mr. Marley, I remember where you live," Jacob said softly, flashing him a dazzling grin in the rearview mirror. "It's just . . . time, I suppose . . . that I do what I'm here for."

A cold chill ran through Eben at those obscure words. "You're my driver, that's what you're here for. Now take me home, if you like your job."

Jacob chuckled, a deep, rolling laugh that probably invited others to laugh with him. "This job? Driving you around? No—I don't care for it, in particular. Wouldn't be a bad one, heaven knows it's easy enough. Except you have got to be the coldest man I've ever met in my life. And it's been a long one."

Eben's eyes narrowed and he said, "Jacob, you are pushing it."

The driver laughed. "Boy, you are the one who's been pushing it. And you're too damned stupid to even know it, all that money, that brain of yours . . . shoot, you're even a good-looking kid," Jacob mused, shaking his head slightly as he took an exit that led even farther away from Eben's home. They were close to Louisville Metro's city limits now, and home was a good twenty miles away.

"Why, thank you. Now turn this fucking car around, take me home, and I'll cut your check. Your final one," Eben snapped, furious.

Jacob continued on as if Eben hadn't spoken. "Smart, rich, and you're good with people, when you want to be. Yet you're concerned with one thing, and one thing only. Yourself. But that's okay. That's why we're here. To open your eyes. Hold on."

Eben opened his mouth to bellow . . . but Jacob wasn't there. The front seat was empty.

"Mother fuck!" Eben shouted, diving over the seat in a desperate attempt to catch the steering wheel.

The car smashed into something, and Eben went flying through the windshield. How odd . . . it didn't even hurt . . .

Damn it . . . why now? he wondered, and then blackness—

2

D amn it, she was so sweet, so hot . . . Eben groaned
as she levered up away from him, laving his cock
with one last gentle stroke of her tongue before she
crawled over him, one knee on each side of his hips.

She stared at him as she held his cock steady with one hand,
her fingers pale and small against the ruddy flesh of his sex.
Eben swore his heart was going to stop in his chest as she
slowly lowered herself down over him, taking his dick deep
inside the wet, swollen depths of her pussy.

Seating herself fully on him, she planted her hands against
his chest, her head falling back. Eben thought his heart was
going to explode as she arched her back, the motion thrusting
her breasts up, the dark pink nipples tight and beaded.

His cock jerked as she started to move, slowly, lazily, the
muscles in her pussy closing around him hot and snug. As she

worked herself up and down on his length, Eben cupped the firm flesh of her ass in his hands.

Sleek, sexy . . . she was so damned hot, he thought she'd burn him alive. The air was heavy with the scent of her aroused body, a light sheen of sweat covering her supple curves. He shuddered as she slid up, then down, a fiery trickle of her cream burning his balls as it flowed down.

Damn it, I could fuck her for the rest of my life and never get tired of her, he thought mindlessly.

A soft, silken voice purred into his mind, Then why did you send her away?

He jerked awake, viciously, abruptly, his cock throbbing against his belly, pulsating and aching like a bad tooth. His heart was pounding hard and heavy. And he hurt.

Oh, hell . . . he hurt. As the dream fell apart around him, Eben grew aware of just how badly he was hurting. And not just his swollen dick, either.

Head pounding, gut churning, body screaming at him in protest, Eben lifted his head, trying to see around him. Too damn dark . . . What in the hell had happened?

He'd been dreaming, that much he knew. Dreaming about Cara. Again.

But what had happened? Where in the hell was he? Not at home, that was for sure. And why the hell couldn't he see anything?

Jacob . . . driving . . . Where in the hell had he been going?

The pain in his head rose up, damn near drowning him, overwhelming the heat from the dream. As the lust-induced fog started to clear, Eben became even more aware of his pounding head. He pressed a hand to his temple, hesitantly, almost afraid he'd find his skull split open. But there were no bumps, no cuts, no wetness that might indicate he was bleeding.

And he could feel his body. Could move—although he sure as hell didn't want to.

What had happened? He didn't remember anything beyond climbing into the car with Jacob—

Jacob had been driving—shit, where in the hell is he?

But it was so black, he couldn't see. It wasn't even the black of night. It was the black of a cave, deep in the depths of the earth, the total absence of any light. "Jacob?" he tried to call.

But his voice was barely a whisper. Licking his lips, he started to pat his pockets. There was a light on his cell phone . . . He could use it to find Jacob . . .

Memory rushed back and he froze.

Shit.

Jacob had disappeared. Right in front of Eben's eyes, right after the man had said, Hold on.

"Son of a bitch!" Eben groaned, fisting his hand and slamming it down . . . and down . . . and down . . . There was nothing under him. No bed, no ground, no rock floor. Nothing.

And as his mind tried to wrap itself around that concept, he started to fall.

A harsh curse escaped him, his body tensing with fear. Arms flailing, he tried to grab onto something, to anything. But there was nothing there.

And still, he continued to fall, his clothes flapping around him, his hair streaming into his eyes, the wind striking his face.

Down and down, until his descent finally seemed to slow, and his clothes stopped flapping. That was the first sign that he might be slowing down—his clothes drifting loosely around him, his hair blowing around his face instead of slapping and stinging his skin and eyes.

A few moments later, his feet landed on the ground. Eben blinked. There was light now, bright blinding light, where moments before, there had been none. It grew brighter and brighter as he stared into it, until, like the sun, it eclipsed, and the light softened.

Now a warm, amber glow cast its light on everything.

Finally able to see, Eben turned and looked around him. He was in a room. Or he thought he was, although there were no doors, no windows. And when he looked up, trying to see where he had fallen from—just a ceiling, a domed, smooth shape that stretched maybe twenty feet over his head.

Bad enough that he'd fallen, now he couldn't see where he'd fallen from. He could have handled that. And he could have figured out how to explain his being in this room, although there was clearly no way out. Like he had been put in a box as the box was being constructed around him.

Yes, he could handle that. Figure it out. Deal with it.

But the soft laughter that was echoing through the room, that was a little harder to understand.

Because he knew that laugh.

And the person it belonged to was dead.

"Well, son, you never were one for listening, were you, Eben?"

Slowly, afraid his ears were playing tricks on him, he turned around.

And sitting there, twenty feet away, settled on a couch exactly like that one Eben had found him on the day he'd died, was Eben's father.

Rustily, he said, "Okay, what's going on? Is this some kind of sick joke?"

Taylor Marley laughed again, shaking his head, flashing that familiar old smile. "No, son. Not a joke. It's just me, your dad," he said, smiling at Eben, a smile that seemed bittersweet.

"Not possible. You died. More than fifteen years ago," Eben said flatly, shaking his head. "What in the hell is going on? Who in the hell are you? Did somebody hire you and that bastard, Jacob? You two playing some weird kind of joke?"

"Well, now, that's not a nice thing to say," Taylor said, his mouth twisting into a frown as he stared at Eben. "Jacob isn't a bastard—he's one of the finest men I've met since I came here. And I've met quite a few outstanding individuals."

"Awww, now that's okay," a low, deep voice said, that southern accent as musical as it had been when he was telling Eben to hold on.

Eben whirled, forgetting that his body had been screaming at him moments before, forgetting the pounding in his head.

Forgetting everything but the man who was standing in front of him, staring at him with those dark, dark brown eyes and a friendly smile. Pointing at him, Eben said, "Jacob, you're lucky I don't kick your ass right here. Get me the hell out of here. Now."

"Oh, in good time," Jacob said, smiling.

"In good time," his father echoed.

Eben finally stopped pacing, a growl of frustration ripping from his throat. No damned way out . . . no way in that he could see. So how had they gotten in here? Blowing out a soft breath, he decided that didn't matter.

What mattered was getting out.

So he tamped down the anger and the fear he was feeling and went to stand before his father, ignoring the man seated in the armchair next to them, playing solitaire. "What in the hell am I doing here?" he asked without preamble.

Taylor laughed and clapped his hands together. "Damn, it's about time," he said. Then his face sobered and he leaned back, staring at Eben with inscrutable brown eyes. "Did you forget what I told you?"

Don't waste your life . . .

His father's last words to him echoed through Eben's mind, even as he searched his memory, trying to figure out what in the hell his old man was getting at.

"Well, that's an improvement, at least. You admit he is your father and this isn't a joke," Jacob mused, slowly turning over another card and tossing it down before lifting his gaze to meet Eben's.

Eben's eyes flew wide and he whispered, "What?"

"You heard me. And yes, for the record, I can read your mind . . . sometimes." Jacob crossed his arms over his chest, leaning back to stare at Eben with shrewd eyes. "As can your father."

Taylor lifted a brow at Eben and sighed tiredly. "Boy, I tried to tell ya, then. And you didn't listen," he said quietly, leaning his head back.

Eben said forcefully, "I don't know what you are talking about. I'm done with this. Take me home."

"You do know what I'm talking about. I told you not to waste your life," Taylor snapped, standing up and stalking away from them, going to stare at a blank wall. "Don't go trying to search that steel trap of a mind, looking for some other reason. Not when you know damned good and well what I'm talking about. You. Wasting your life."

"I'm not," Eben said, startled by the vague, accusatory glance Taylor Marley shot him. "Damn it, I run a multimillion-dollar advertising business, have a vacation home in California and one in France. I was—"

Taylor waved his hand and spat, "Bah! It means nothing . . . because you are empty. When was the last time you were truly happy?"

Eben stilled. He blinked, staring at his father as those words echoed in his mind. Then he shook his head and said, "I am happy."

Empty . . . The word resonated through him. Empty. He clenched his jaw, and through gritted teeth spat, "I am happy."

"You're not," Jacob said from behind them.

Eben turned and demanded, "How in the hell would you know? You're my driver—or you were. I'm firing your ass."

Okay, Eben . . . buddy, you're sounding crazy. You know this isn't really happening.

Taylor had lifted his eyes skyward and was murmuring

silently to himself when Eben looked back at him. A deep, weary sigh escaped the older Marley as he leaned forward, pinning his son with an intense, stark stare. "Boy, this is really happening. Deal with it. As to firing Jacob, well, he's already got a pretty good job. I think he'll do okay without yours."

Jacob chuckled, a deep, rolling sound that echoed in the room. "That's the truth. Though I don't know much about earthly ways anymore, I suppose the pay was pretty good. But the atmosphere sucked." He lifted a black brow at him and smiled.

Eben couldn't stop the flush that heated his face. Sucked, did it? "Well, that will teach me to let employees have half days off on Christmas Eve."

Jacob laughed, lifting his face to the sky as he murmured, "You are clueless, aren't you?"

Taylor sighed sadly as Eben opened his mouth, closed it, opened it again as he tried to think of what to say to that last comment. "It's my fault, Jacob. I should have raised him a little better, made him understand there's more to life than money, than working. Of course, I didn't really understand that until I met Liz. My sweet angel . . . I miss her."

"Isn't she here with you?" Eben asked. Then he smacked himself in the forehead. "Hell, I'm actually believing this. What is wrong with me?"

Taylor smiled at him. "Relax, son. It's going to be okay—I think," his father said. "Liz is with me—just not here. I've been watching you for the past few months, pretty closely. And she couldn't come. It was tough leaving her, but this is important."

Eben spread his hands and demanded, "What's important? What's going on? What in the hell am I doing here?" Then an awful thought occurred to him and he paled, flinching instinctively as the possibility reared its ugly head. "Am I . . . dead?"

"No, son, but you're running out of time. Either live as you should or keep going down the path you're going. And end up alone and lonely," Taylor said.

Jacob said quietly from behind them, "Listen to your daddy, Eben. Clock's ticking. You've got tonight, and then we just walk away. No more chances. And son, without somebody hitting you in the head with a two-by-four, or disappearing in a car right in front of you, you aren't going to try to be different. Not on your own. You've lived like this for more than twenty-five years, and if you haven't changed by now . . . Well, you aren't going to rediscover life at age fifty-five like Marley Sr. did."

Sweat beading on his brow, Eben asked, "What do you mean I have tonight?"

Taylor was silent, cocking a brow at Jacob. The black man crossed his arms in front of him and pursed his lips, lowering his brows, reminding Eben for some odd reason of Sidney Poitier in the movie Sneakers. His dark face was serious, solemn, and his eyes just as penetrating as the actor's.

"You have tonight. A chance to look back over your life and see if you're really living it the way you want. After tonight, you'll have a choice, to be more than what you are. Or just keep going. If you choose that, that's fine. We won't interfere anymore. But there will come a time, and possibly very soon, when you will regret the choices you've made in life."

Hell, I already do. Hiring you, Eben thought sourly. "So what am I supposed to do tonight?" he asked, jamming his hands into the deep pockets of his coat.

"Just watch . . . and listen. You'll have some guides. Just go where they tell you, and listen to what they have to say," Taylor said, smiling gently.

"And if I don't?" Eben asked, cocking a brow at his father. "If I'm happy as I am?"

"Well, you don't have much choice about whether or not you go with them tonight. You will go," Taylor said flatly. "But after that, if you really think this existence of yours can be called happy—so be it."

"You will have three guides—"

Eben interrupted Jacob with a laugh. "Three guides. Oh, hell, this is good. Three guides," he muttered, shaking his head. "You know, with my name, I thought I'd heard every joke about the Christmas Carol and old Scrooge imaginable. But this is definitely new."

Eben spun around and plowed his fingers through his hair, staring off into the amber light that surrounded them. "Look, Dad, it's not that I don't appreciate your concern, but—"

A deep peal of sound echoed through the room and darkness fell once more, hiding everything from sight.

"Dad!" Eben called out, searching his pockets frantically for his cell phone. Silence . . . no answer. "Dad!"

He finally found the damn phone and tried to remember by touch alone where on the dial pad the button for the mini flashlight was located. But before he could find it, the darkness lifted and he was standing on the street where he grew up.

Only that wasn't possible. They had torn that neighborhood down and put in a golf course. Years ago. So how in the hell could he be seeing it now?

His eyes alit on a small boy, wispy blond hair falling into his eyes, the thick lenses covering them magnifying his eyes to damn near twice their normal size.

Holy shit!

"You were such a sweet kid, you know that?"

Eben blinked, his corrected vision graying for a second. Then he turned, his eyes widening as he stared at a statuesque, lushly built woman. Damn, talk about a wet dream . . .

She wore a wine-red robe of velvet, the real kind, his experienced eye decided, with that luster that only silk velvet had. The velvet gleamed richly against the deep cleavage revealed by the plunging neckline. Her skin looked satiny, touchably soft, and Eben felt his fingers itch to touch, for just a minute. Thick black hair waved down past her full hips, and nestled in the dense black waves was a crown made of flowers and . . . fruit?

The woman's eyes were a deep, fathomless blue, and they twinkled as she stared down at him. And she did have to look down—she must have been nearly seven feet tall.

Eben was about five-ten, so he felt like a damned midget, much like he had felt through most of high school, until he'd finally shot up from his five-two skinny stature. Well, he had still been skinny, until he'd started swimming and running, finally developing some muscle.

Not that he had a bad view from here—he was on eye level with a very nice, very round set of breasts, and he could smell the seductively sweet scent of her body.

"Ahem."

He tore his eyes away from that lovely set of tits and met

her gaze, seeing the laughter lurking there. "I'd be offended, if I wasn't so pleased to actually see a human reaction from you," she said, her deep, throaty voice caressing his ears, stirring his blood. "You so easily ignore women, ignore life . . . ignore everything but the money you love to make. Well, there was one woman who made you feel human . . . but we'll get to her later."

As she laughed again, Eben scowled, turning away. That deep chuckle echoed in his ears as he stared at the boy—the long forgotten image of himself as a child. That was back before Mama had left them, running off to be with her rich lover. Eben had learned years later that she had died in a car wreck after she and that bastard had partied it up too much just a few months after she'd left them.

He hadn't known—his dad had figured he'd been through too much trauma already for a five-year-old, losing his mama once. He didn't need to lose her again. "That's me, isn't it?" he asked, his voice oddly husky.

"Yes, it is," she said. Long moments passed as they watched the boy. When she broke the silence again, her voice was soft and gentle as she told him, "I'm your guide."

He snorted. "I figured you were going to say that. Do we really have to live this entire Dickens charade through?"

Again, she laughed, lifting her face to the sun. "It's been a long while since I thought of him," she murmured, a soft smile curving up the corners of that wide, sexy mouth.

"Dickens?"

"No, Ebenezer Scrooge. You share a great deal in common with him—not just your name," she said gently, her eyes softening as she watched the boy stand up, cradling a model aircraft precariously in his hands. "Such a remarkable boy, you were, so smart, so quick. He was, too."

"He who?"

"Why, Ebenezer Scrooge, of course," she replied, the expression on her lovely face saying that he should already know that.

"That's a fictional character," Eben said, rolling his eyes.

"Hmmm . . . are you so certain?" the guide asked, winking at him. "I remember him rather well. You are so like he was . . . but you are a great deal younger. Too young to be so cynical."

Eben shook his head, at a loss for words. Now he was being told one of the great works of classic literature was based on truth. That was ridiculous. He cocked his head, watching the boy as he carried the model airplane up the sidewalk to the porch of the house. "I wanted to be a pilot," he murmured.

"Yes—I believe you would have been a remarkable one," she mused.

In the blink of an eye, they were at the window of the house, staring in. Eben watched with reluctant fascination as one of the most hurtful memories of his childhood played out before him. Eyes shining, the young child proudly displayed the aircraft to his father, and was rebuffed. His father was too intent on his books, his files, his notes, barely glancing at the model as he scowled. "Ben, I've no time for your toys and foolishness. I have to . . ."

The words faded into the distance as Eben watched the child image of him deflate. "Five-year-olds generally can't do models by themselves," he said thickly. "I tried to get Dad to help me—but he was too busy."

"Hmmm, I know, sweetie," the guide murmured, lifting a

long, graceful hand to rest on his shoulder. "You rarely played with toys, did you?"

"There was no point. Toys didn't do anything," he said, his voice husky. Why were his eyes stinging? He wanted, badly, to go up to that boy and hug him close.

"Your father did love you," she said quietly. "He was just hurting so terribly inside."

"Hell, it was just an airplane," he muttered, shaking his head tiredly, blinking away that peculiar stinging in his eyes.

"Was it?" she asked.

The image before them faded away, replaced by an image of an older Eben, one bent low over his books, his young face tightening with a scowl as a merry laugh echoed out. "Eben, all you do is study!"

Bella . . . his throat tightened. Damn it, he hadn't thought of her in years.

As he watched, the younger Ebenezer Marley lifted his head from his books, his thin face drawing tight in a scowl as he stared at his high school girlfriend. Why hadn't he realized how lucky he was to have her? Girls like that never looked twice at scholarly geeks like him.

With her long, thick butter-yellow curls, and sparkling blue eyes, Bella Martin was a high school boy's dream come true— slender, svelte, open. So kind, so sweet, and she had wanted him.

"C'mon, let's go sledding. The snow from last night is perfect—we can go out to Morgan's Hill and sled, then go to Beth's and have some hot chocolate, watch movies," she said, kneeling down by him, running her fingers through his hair, her eyes imploring.

"I don't have time for that foolishness right now, Bella. I've got to get these papers done so I can turn them in after the break. I'll be graduating early, and I've got too much to get done to play," he said dismissively, moving his head away from the distracting caress of her hand.

The boy hadn't seen the look on her face. But the man watching them now saw, and he felt it like a punch in the gut. "That's was kind of shitty of me," he whispered, his heart clenching as her pretty blue eyes filled with tears, not just at his refusal to go and have fun with her, but from the way he moved away from her touch.

She probably wouldn't have understood that it didn't irritate him, it was distracting. Her touch, her laugh, the sweet way she smelled made him want to forget everything, and just be with her.

Her lips trembled and she sighed, her voice whisper soft as she said, "Okay, Eben. I guess I can go alone."

"Why in the hell didn't I just go with her?" he muttered, his eyes hard and grim as he stared at the downward angle of his head, the young Eben so focused on his books.

"Much like you are now," she said shrewdly. "Isn't he? Focused on nothing more than studying, while you focus on making money. You don't even spend that much of it. You hoard it. What are you saving it for?"

"Money's too hard to come by to spend it recklessly," he said absently, unaware of how his hand kept rubbing over his chest, right over the ache in his heart.

"Not for you," she countered. "You make money almost as easy as you breathe. When it comes to the business world, everything you touch turns to gold, doesn't it, Ebenezer?"

He shot her a narrow look. "Don't call me that," he said shortly as the world around them faded away, enshrouded in fog.

"Ahhh, you've always hated that name, haven't you? Eben or Ben, doesn't matter which one people call you, as long as it's not Ebenezer." She flashed him a grin, her full ruby-red lips parting to reveal a dazzling white smile. "Not that I blame you. The name does sound like it belongs to an old man. Can't understand why your mama named you that."

A cruel joke, he thought sourly, his eyes dropping to the lush mouth of the guide. Then he jerked away, spinning around.

And stared at yet another scene from his past. "No." His voice flat, firm and decisive, he shook his head and repeated, "No. I don't want to see this."

As Bella, older now, her face sadder, stared off into the distance, Eben, now twenty-five and already rich, glared at her. "You're what?" he repeated, dismayed.

"I'm getting married," she said quietly. "I met him in France. Remember, you couldn't go with me, too busy." She shrugged, but he could see the echo of pain in her eyes. Now.

Then, all he had seen was her turning away from him. "Damn it, how in the hell can you be getting married? We're supposed to be getting married."

She gave a watery laugh and asked, "When? First it was after college, then it was after I got a higher paying job at a better school. I've been teaching at Country Day for two years now, Eben. And we haven't even set a date. Now you want to get this buyout done, then we can talk about it. But after that, something else will come up, and I'm tired of coming in behind your desire to make money, baby. I need to come first, for once."

Eben's former self arrogantly said, "You do. Why in the hell do you think I'm working so hard? It's for you, for us."

She smiled sadly. "No, Eben," she said gently, her eyes sparkling with the tears she'd held back for years. "It's for you. I don't need millions of dollars to be happy. All I ever needed was you. Once. Now I need to be away from you. I'll never be happy until I'm free of you—because you'll never be free enough for us to be together, get married, have a family."

Eben's belly tightened with disgust as he watched, knowing what was coming next. "Damn it, can he make you feel like I do?" he demanded, striding over to her, cupping her neck and arching her face up, savaging her mouth as he ran knowledge-able hands over her.

They'd lost their virginities together, and he knew that lithe, toned body like the back of his hand. She whimpered in her throat, her hands fisted at his chest. When she finally tore her mouth away, Eben could see the tears streaming down her face. Both the man he had been, and the man he was now, watched as she turned her face away and whispered, "No, Eben, it's over."

As she walked away from him, the fog closed in, hiding his past self from his view, but the memory of how he looked, shoulders slumped, eyes closed in defeat, lingered. "She would have come back to me, right up until the very last, wouldn't she?" he asked, his voice husky.

The guide sighed, shaking her head as she looked at him. "I don't know, Eben," she said honestly. "Bella loved you, with all her heart. Until your carelessness smashed it, time after time."

The fog lifted and he was now staring in through the window of his penthouse, as he brought woman after woman home with him for a few hours, but never the same woman twice. With every woman he fucked, he sought a replacement for the one he'd lost, and he never found one. Never found anybody that touched something inside him the way Bella had.

Until one night . . . Damn it. She would make him watch this.

As he stared at an image of himself lying beneath a sweet-faced girl, he flushed. Cara . . .

"Ah, yes," the guide murmured, a smug, pleased little smile curving her lips as she glanced from the scene in front of them to Eben. "There's the girl. Even more than Bella, she made you forget yourself, didn't she? So much so that you pushed her away."

"Stop it," he growled, staring at the image of himself in bed with Cara. His gut clenched, his cock jerked in remembered ecstasy as he watched himself slide his hands up the long line of her torso to cup her breasts. He could remember how she felt under his hands . . . soft, silken . . . perfect.

There had been love in her eyes, naked and shining. That girl had been an assistant in accounting, and had been pro-moted after just a few months to an admin assistant. For the past few months, she had been working pretty closely with him, and always staring at him with those pretty green eyes. He gave in to temptation one night—taking her to the Grand, wining and dining her—then he had fucked her silly.

The following Monday he'd had her transferred to another

department, one where he wasn't likely to see her often, if at all.

Just so he wouldn't have to see that love again.

The final image of her was the one he had shut out of his mind, right as he'd closed the door to the suite on her, after telling her Tom would take her home. She had just sat there, staring at him, her pretty green eyes blank.

The guide whispered, "What is it about love that frightens you so, Eben?"

He went stiff as another scene from his past wavered into view, his eyes narrowing on the image of yet another woman—this one somebody he couldn't even remember. How could he forget a woman who had taken his cock into her mouth? A woman whose thighs he had spread wide while he lapped at her pussy? How is that possible? But he had done it. Slowly, carefully, trying to keep the frustration he felt from surfacing in his voice, he said, "Love doesn't frighten me. It's just . . . useless."

"Useless," the spirit repeated, her voice flat and cool. "Love moves mountains, shatters lives and rebuilds them. Love is the most amazing, and sometimes, the most awful thing known to man. Only love could take a child who was raised by cruel parents and turn him into one of the kindest, giving men. Only love could teach a woman who had known only abuse at the hands of a man, to trust another man, and allow him to teach her true pleasure. Love is many things, but never useless."

Eben turned to scowl at her, only to find himself alone. Once more.

3

When he looked back, he was staring through yet another window . . . and this time at Bella. She'd cut her hair.

That was the first thing he noticed. But then he promptly forgot as he realized what she held.

A baby, a tiny, towheaded baby with thick, golden curls, lashes lying low over smooth cheeks as the babe suckled at Bella's breast.

A deep, warm voice murmured, "See what you gave up?"

Unable to turn and meet this new guide, Eben ignored the spirit as he stared at Bella's face, at the happiness he saw there. His throat locked up as she started to sing quietly, rocking back and forth ever so slightly. She'd always had the most amazing voice . . . Swallowing, he whispered, "This isn't real."

Why did staring at the baby nursing wrench at his heart so painfully?

"Oh, it's real, all right," that voice behind him murmured. "The baby is three months old today. His name is Cameron. And he has a sister who is just barely two."

Two? Whirling, eyes lifted, he opened his mouth to rail at the woman in front of him. Only to still, his hand falling to his side as he stared at the exact opposite of the creature who had just left him. Five feet, maybe, reed slender, her mouth painted the color of cherries, her dark chocolate gaze curious, even friendly, as she stared at him. Soft black curls fell into her eyes, over the warm mocha hue of her skin.

She smiled at him sunnily. "Not Morgan, am I?" she teased, that deep throaty voice seeming so at odds with the petite, wraithlike creature in front of him.

"Morgan?" he repeated dumbly.

"Yeah, that tall lady you were just talking to?" she drawled, rolling her eyes at him before sauntering forward. "The Amazon?"

She propped her arms on the windowsill, staring in at Bella. Softly, she said, "She's happy, you know. She rarely even thinks about you, but when she does, she prays. Prays you'll find happiness in your life. But she doesn't even miss you—ain't that sad?"

Absently, he corrected, "Isn't. Isn't that sad?" But he barely even realized he had spoken as he stared in at Bella.

The woman laughed merrily, the rich music of it echoing all around him. "Isn't that sad? I'm trying to teach you an important lesson in life, and you want to correct my grammar," she said, chuckling, her eyes dancing with mirth. "Something is so wrong with that."

Eben scrunched his eyes shut and whispered, "A dream. All

a dream and I'll wake up in bed." He frantically hoped, prayed, and wasted his time, because when he popped one eye open, it was to see the second guide—the spirit—staring at him with bright, curious eyes. She slapped him on the arm and said, "Calm down, babe. You're gonna wake up, in bed even. Question is . . . how long are you going to wake up alone? Wake up lonely, convinced that every ill in life is soothed by the making of money, more and more money? You don't even spend it!"

She smiled, greedily rubbing her hands together. "Damn, if I had some of that money, a real body again, and two hours, that's all I'd need, two hours," she said, wiggling elegantly arched brows at him.

"A-again?" he repeated.

With a whimsical smile, she turned her eyes to him, lifting one small shoulder in a shrug. "I'm dead, Ebenezer. A ghost. What is a ghost, or a spirit, but somebody who died?" She sighed, shaking her head. "But even I lived a better life than you. I was nineteen when I died in that crash. Nineteen. And at least I understood what happy was." She shot his long, expensive wool coat a derisive glance. "It wasn't about money, although I did love to spend it."

Sourly, he snapped, "If you are so wise, then show me, damn it. What in the hell is happy? I want this over with."

Those brows rose above her expressive eyes as she cocked her head at him. Without a single word, she lifted a slender arm and gestured, the filmy white gown she wore floating around her limbs and torso as she turned slightly, stepping out of the way.

Eben felt it in his gut like a vicious punch as he stared back through the window. It was still Bella, only now she held a toddler in her arms . . . and in the toddler's lap was the baby. The little girl was smiling with youthful delight as she ran a finger down the baby's button nose, making him grin and coo. Sitting behind Bella, a contented smile on his face, was the man she had left him for.

Bella's eyes sparkled, a smile of peace and contentment on her face, joy and pride all but radiating from her. And when she lifted her eyes to stare at her husband, a look of lust and love entered them, a small smile curving her lips as she dropped one lid in a quick wink.

The warmth of the room, the happiness that filled it . . . the sound of that little girl laughing made his throat tighten.

Okay.

He got the picture. That was happiness. Tightly, he asked, "Can we go? I see your point. I lost her, lost my chance at that. I'm sorry."

The woman laughed, and this time, it was a sound completely devoid of amusement. "Oh, honey, it's not even close to time for you to go yet."

As the fog moved in, Eben lifted his hand and rested it on the glass between him and Bella, his chest tight.

The glass was still under his palm as the fog cleared, but it had changed. The window was smaller, cramped almost, as he stared through it in bemusement. Who in the hell did he know that lived someplace like this? He was staring through the window into an older home, one that was showing its age despite some valiant attempts to maintain it.

A Christmas tree stood beside a window opposite him, tucked in far too closely to a fireplace. The room was tiny, barely big enough for the tree and the old, run-down couch and a dented, scarred coffee table. Eben turned his head to look at the guide, puzzlement in his eyes. "What are we doing here?"

"You don't know who lives here, do you?" she asked wryly, shaking her head. "I'm not surprised, not really. Although the man worked for you for darn near close to ten years. Tell me something, do you even know his wife's name? His middle name? Whether or not he drank coffee?"

"Who are you talking about?" he demanded, turning his head back to the window, peering through. Cupping his hands around his eyes to shield out the light that emanated from behind him, Eben pressed his face close to the glass. There was a picture on the mantel . . .

A toddler came running in, tripping over her own feet and tumbling to the ground. Throwing her head back, she opened her mouth and let out a loud wail. A man came into view, chuckling as he knelt to lift the baby, holding her against his chest and rocking her. "Shhhh, Katie, it's okay . . . Got a boo-boo? I can kiss it," he murmured.

Daniel Wilson—what in the hell was he doing here?

The man was a former manager of the design department. "I don't get it. What is Dan doing here?"

"Where else would he be on Christmas? He's home, of course, with his family. That's where we all deserve to be on the holidays," the spirit said softly. "Isn't she pretty?"

Eben's eyes were unwittingly drawn to the pretty little girl but he didn't comment about the child. Instead, he said, "I pay my people decent. He was a manager, for crying out loud. He can afford better than this."

"Well, at one time, he had better than this. But he gave it up—somebody he loves is very, very sick . . . and the insurance was changed. To a plan that's barely substandard. He's going broke on medical bills and prescriptions," she said levelly. But Eben could see the displeasure in her eyes.

He felt that look, that disappointment, strike him like a fist in his gut. As guilt and shame started to build inside him, Eben licked his lips. "The insurance policy we used to have was too expensive. We have to keep costs down . . ." But why did the words sound so trite as he looked at one of the sharpest minds he had ever worked with?

Because they were trite. It wouldn't have affected anything, really, not with the kind of business he did, to keep the better insurance plan. But when Martin Shanning had suggested the cheaper one, well, hell, Eben was all for keeping down costs.

Come to think of it, Dan had made a politely voiced complaint about the change. And Eben had ignored him.

A year later, he'd fired him because Dan had refused some business trips that Eben had thought were necessary. "I can't be gone from my family so long," Dan had argued.

"I'm sorry to hear that, Dan. I wish you luck elsewhere."

Just before Thanksgiving.

The door swung open, revealing a slight, pale child, and woman with weary eyes standing behind her. The glass between them seemed to fade as their words suddenly became painfully clear. "Livvy, honey, you aren't supposed to be out of bed," Dan said gently, shifting the toddler to one hip as he moved to the girl with the overlarge eyes, set in a thin, hollow-cheeked face.

She giggled and said, "Daddy, Santa doesn't want me in bed on Christmas. I'm going to flop on the couch. Mama said I could."

"I thought we were going to bring all the presents up to your room," Dan said, stooping down and lifting the frail child in his arms.

"But it's not as much fun without the tree," she said simply, resting her head on her father's shoulder.

As Dan turned, Eben flinched at the look in his eyes, angry, helpless . . . full of love. He looked so tired.

"What's wrong with her?" Eben asked, almost afraid to.

"She has a congenital heart defect. She's always been too ill to try corrective surgery. Asthma, pneumonia . . . The doctors now think she's finally strong enough to try the surgery. But the insurance is balking about covering it," the spirit said, her voice hard and brittle as ice, her eyes going cold and flat as death. "Daniel is working with several groups to raise money. He wanted to try a fundraiser at work—"

Eben clenched his jaw tightly, self-disgust roiling through him as he recalled Daniel approaching him about possibly trying charitable fundraisers—a lot of employees liked to do them, made them feel good about themselves and their workplace.

And Eben's response? "Then they can go work at a homeless shelter on their days off. That's not what the workplace is for."

"I'm a real bastard," Eben whispered, staring at the family through the window, watching as Daniel passed the toddler off to her mama so he could tuck the sick little girl onto the couch, pulling a blanket up to warm her.

"Yes. Of course, firing him right before the holidays really topped it," the guide said brightly, smiling sunnily. But the look in her eyes as she stared at the girl showed him what she was feeling inside.

Helpless, angry . . . much like Daniel looked.

"I'll hire him back," he whispered to himself. Change the insurance, give him a raise . . . He shouldn't have to live in this fucking dump. As the anger churned through him, he asked, "Will it save her? The surgery?"

The spirit shook her head as she sadly said, "Nobody knows. She's got a unique medical problem. The vessels that are supposed to pump the blood to her lungs for oxygen just aren't there. A doctor in Florida thinks he can place vessels there—but it's experimental."

"What about some kind of governmental aid? Won't they cover it?"

"That's where Daniel's gone, finally. His pride wouldn't let him while he was able to do it. But her medical bills are piling up and without a job, he's going to have to declare bankruptcy. And that sort of word will get around. Who wants to hire a guy to help run an ad design department when he can't manage his own finances better than that?"

One had nothing to do with the other, Eben thought, his frustration mounting the longer he stared at the little girl. She was a pretty thing, frail and almost fey; she was so thin. Her eyes sparkled and danced as she tore into her presents with glee, unaware of the looks being passed between mother and father.

"If she doesn't get that surgery, this will be her last Christmas," the spirit whispered at his side, rising onto her toes and resting her hand on Eben's shoulder as she spoke. "They know that, as much as they fight against admitting it. But her time is running out. Daniel wanted her to have the world—and he can barely manage to buy presents for his kids at Christmas."

Eben whirled away, pacing, his hands opening and closing in futile rage. My fault—damn it, this is my fault, he thought, enraged. Spinning around, chin lifted, he demanded, "Take me back. Now. I'll pay for the surgery, I'll pay all the medical bills. I'll give him his job back, with a raise—anything. I can't—"

A knot swelled in his throat, so heavy, so huge, he could barely speak around it.

"I can't—"

The spirit stared at him, her eyes glowing, a tiny smile lurking at her mouth. "Can't what, Ebenezer Marley?" she asked as his voice trailed off.

Turning, he walked back to the window and whispered, "I can't let that little girl die."

She laughed sadly. "Money can't buy everything. All the money in the world won't save her if God decides she's suffered enough." Then she slid him a sidelong glance. "Besides, we're not done yet. There's so much more for you to see."

The fog shrouded them, and then he was staring in through a grand Palladian window, watching the people in the room who were gathered around a white tree, strung with white lights and hung with magnificent golden bows and ornaments. A deep, rollicking laugh echoed through the room, and unconsciously, Eben's own lips curled in response.

The spirit's gaze dropped to his mouth, one raven brow lifting in appraisal.

Eben didn't notice—his eyes were rapt on the man striding past the window, coming to a stop by a small child playing by the tree. "My cousin—Joshua Marley," he murmured. "He asked me to come over for Christmas."

"Yep," the spirit said, a sardonic smile curving her lips. "He sure did. Even though his wife told him not to. She doesn't care for you, Eben."

No. Eben agreed in silence as he watched said wife come into the room, wearing a rich burgundy velvet gown. Tracey couldn't care less for Eben, hadn't been able to think kindly of him since she'd heard he had ordered a thorough investigation of her after Josh had proposed. He'd just been looking out for his cousin—one of his rare sincere acts for somebody other than himself.

But it had been an insult to her, he realized now. She loved Joshua, he thought as she walked up to the huge, bearlike man and wrapped her arms around him, smiling up at him.

"You haven't heard from Eben, have you, Tracey?" Joshua asked, stooping down to lift the boy into his arms.

"No, baby," Tracey said, rolling her eyes before she leaned over and kissed Joshua on the cheek. "You need to just give up on that guy, Josh. He doesn't care about anybody but himself and his money."

"Now, Trace," Josh said, sighing, shaking his head.

She held up a hand, eyes closing for just a second. "I'm sorry. You're right—just because he's a cold, calculating bastard doesn't mean we should think uncharitable thoughts toward him," she said flippantly.

"That wasn't exactly what I was thinking," Josh said, chuckling. "But . . . Eben's a lonely guy. I bet he doesn't even realize how lonely he is."

Tracey smiled warmly up at Joshua, wrapping her arms around him. "Hmmm . . . and he thinks he's the rich one," she whispered. "We've got so much more than he'll ever have."

"I'm not giving up on him," Joshua murmured.

Outside, Eben felt his throat tighten, his eyes stinging. Thanks, Josh. "He's a good guy," he murmured to the spirit. Only she wasn't there.

A chill ran through Eben as the glowing light dimmed, and the air around him grew colder and colder.

A whisper of sound ran through the air, a sighing—deep, desolate, and cold. Indeed . . . a voice whispered, the word seeming to come from everywhere and nowhere at the same time.

He is the only one who would truly mourn you, if suddenly you were gone.

Eben whirled around, staring into the thick gray fog, trying to find who was speaking. "Where are you?" he demanded, his heart slamming against his ribs.

The wind whistled, blowing at his coat, whipping his hair around his face as he peered into the grayness.

Well . . . perhaps this is another.

The voice was low, with an odd, almost hissing sound, slithering against his skin, and the sound of it made melancholy rise within him. As the fog lifted, he saw a woman—with a short, sleek cap of black hair, a spiky fringe of bangs falling into a pair of green eyes that had been laughing the last time he saw them.

The time before that? Blank, empty . . . right before he'd closed the door and summoned his driver to pick her up from the hotel.

It was Cara, her head bent low against the wind, her shoulders slumped, grief etched onto her face. There was just sadness now, no husky laugh that drew people to her, invited them to laugh with her, no wicked smile. Just grief.

Why would she miss him?

You have a talent . . . for making people love you, without even trying. And then you destroy it. Those last words were whispered with a low, mean hiss that sent shivers down his spine.

This newest spirit didn't like him—the others may have been disappointed, but this one had a rampant dislike of him. Eben could feel it.

A cold, cruel laugh echoed around him and just behind him, to the side, right at the edge of his peripheral vision, he saw somebody move. Turning, he found himself staring at a hooded figure. It was a woman. Under that spidery gossamer weave of her gown, he saw a woman's form—firm, small breasts, sleek hips, long thighs—but her face was obscured by the hood. All he could see was the cold blue gleam of her eyes.

"On the contrary," the guide murmured, and her voice was that chilling rasp that made his skin crawl. "I like you, and people like you, quite a lot. People like you always come to me with a scream of disbelief, as though you cannot understand why in the world you landed in my cold, desolate domain."

Eben swallowed, squinting as he tried to discern the face within that enveloping cloak. "Are you the final spirit?" he asked in a low, gritty voice.

"Indeed. Look at the woman you could have had—if you had just offered a simple smile," the guide whispered, holding out a slim, pale hand and pointing.

For a long moment, he couldn't even move—her skin was translucent. He could see the shadow of the bones that made up her hand. Shaken, he lifted his eyes and stared back at Cara's lowered head, his eyes tracking where she stared.

A gravestone.

She was standing at a grave—

Holy shit!

Somebody called her name and Cara lifted her head, letting Eben see the sparkle of tears in her eyes. Somebody came trudging up through the snow covering the ground. The guy was familiar, but Eben couldn't place him.

"What are you doing here, Cara?" the guy asked, staring down at the headstone, his body blocking it from view.

"Doug, go away," she said, her voice weary.

"I want to know, damn it. We've been going out for three months. I don't like this obsession you have with a dead guy."

Cara lifted her eyes, her chin going up. "We stopped dating three weeks ago. I broke it off, remember?" she said coolly. Then she moved her eyes back to the headstone. "And I can't explain my obsession, as you call it. There was just—something about him. He called to me."

Those words faded away as Cara's form slowly faded away.

Eben was left staring at the headstone.

But he didn't need to see it. He already knew it was his name.

Today's date was on it. December 24, 2004.

"If I'm supposed to be dead, why are you showing me this?" he asked, his voice shuddering out of him as a dull, leaden weight settled in his heart.

"That is yet to be seen," she said obscurely. "There's another grave here—somebody you've seen before."

Eben lifted his head with dread. "No."

As he watched Daniel walk across the lonely, empty grave-yard, Eben's heart started to bleed—black, bitter blood that he felt spreading through his veins with every beat of his worth-less heart.

"Not the girl," he whispered, the hot sting of tears in his eyes. "I don't want to see this!" he bellowed, whirling away. But in every direction he turned, he saw the same tableau playing out before him, Daniel walking alone through the snow-covered cemetery, a gay red poinsettia in his arm, his face lined and weary. He looked twenty years older.

"She died on the table. It took a while for him to raise the money and she caught ill, again. But her heart was failing—they waited months for her to get stronger, and she never did. They decided to take the chance," the spirit said, her voice deepening, and starting to echo. "They lost."

A whisper of a sigh escaped the guide and she said, "The girl is not here though—she went on. The young and the goodhearted usually do."

"Went on?"

The ghost replied, "Of course . . . to there."

Eben followed the direction she was pointing, that long, pale hand with its ghastly imagery of bones visible. His throat swelled as he saw a soft, golden light gleaming in the distance, far away.

"Indeed, very far, for one such as you," she whispered.

Eben's legs went out and he fell to his knees in front of the gravestone that bore his name.

"Tell me you're lying, that the girl didn't die," he said flatly, his heart aching as he looked from that soft golden light back to Daniel.

"She was a weak child, Eben—too weak." Something in her voice made him look up, the echo of grief, the huskiness of tears.

"No," he whispered, thickly, shaking his head.

"No."

4

No.

    No.

    No.

The words echoed inside his head. The darkness surrounding him was heavy and oppressive. As Eben finally forced his eyes to open, he found himself lying in his own bed, his eyes on the elaborate metalwork that made up the canopy.

He jerked up, his breath sawing in and out of his lungs in harsh, ragged gasps.

What in the hell?

A dream . . . just a dream . . .

"No, Ebenezer Marley, it's not," said a familiar voice from over by the window.

He jerked his gaze around, eyes widening as he saw

Jacob standing there, a pocketknife in one hand, a chunk of wood in the other. "Not a dream," Jacob mused as he started to whittle on the piece of wood, brows drawn low in concentration.

"You." Eben pressed his hands to his eyes, trying to convince himself he really wasn't shaking. No reason to be shaking, it was a dream.

Jacob chuckled. "Your dad warned me you'd be stubborn," he mused, shaking his head. Lifting those sharp, intelligent eyes, he said quietly, "It's Christmas Eve, and you have some choices . . ."

Rolling out of bed, Eben stood naked in the cool air, staring out the window of his grand home—over the lonely estate—as snow started to fall.

Why hadn't he ever realized how lonely it was?

Jacob's chuckle was just a memory in the air as Eben strode to his closet, jerking open the doors and grabbing the first things that came to hand, blue jeans and a heavy sweater, lying folded on a shelf.

And on top of them, he found a small piece of wood, carved into the shape of a child, kneeling by a bed, hands folded in prayer. Carved in tiny letters into the footboard was a word . . . Choices . . .

Choices . . . closing his eyes, he remembered that split second of fear that he had squashed as he went flying through the window.

Why now?

As he stared at the small carving, the answer to that question came to him.

Because he had been walking into a very dim, very lackluster future, a cold, empty one. And he'd never even realized it. He had to wonder, even if he had realized it, would it have mattered?

As a thousand thoughts raced through his head, another question passed through his mind. Why not sooner?

Because up until just now . . . he didn't think it would have mattered.

Folding his hand around the wood, he held onto it as he jerked his jeans on. Then he tucked it safely into his pocket before yanking the sweater over his head.

Moments later, he was on the phone with his personal assistant, an older, soft-spoken woman by the name of Clarise. She said quietly, "I certainly hope you're feeling better. It's so unlike you to be ill—and so close to the holidays . . . That's terrible."

"Ill?" he repeated.

"Hmmm. I was rather surprised when you called me so late last night, but if you hadn't, I would have worried when you didn't come to work. You needn't worry, sir. Everything here is fine—"

What in the hell? he muttered silently, shaking his head. "Listen, I need some information about a former employee, Daniel Wilson. His address, for starters. And then every known debt that he has. And come tomorrow—no, tomorrow is Christmas—come Monday, I want every single debt paid off. Use my personal company account and say nothing to him about it."

There was silence on the other end of the phone. Then, a

polite clearing of the throat. "Sir? You want me to pay off his debts?"

"Yes. All of them. And get me the name of the top pediatric cardiologist in the country. No. In the world. I want the best. And soon. Call me on my cell phone—I have some Christmas shopping to do."

On the other end of the line, he was unaware of the shock on Clarise's face as she repeated faintly, "Christmas shopping?"

He had already hung up the phone, striding out of his bedroom as he made sure he had his cell phone. "Jacob!"

Bea, his butler, slid out of a room. A puzzled look in her eyes, she said, "Sir? Is there something you need?"

"Yes. Where is Jacob?"

She frowned, cocking her head at him. Finally, she asked, "Ahhh . . . Jacob? Sir, I don't know any Jacob."

"My driver," Eben said with a frown, staring at her in puzzlement. "I hired him a few weeks ago."

Bea shifted from one foot to the other, looking as distressed as he had ever seen her. "Sir, you've been driving yourself for the past month. Ever since you let Tom go." And although her expression never changed and her voice remained level, Eben could feel the cool displeasure that action had earned him.

"Driving myself?" he repeated. Hell, maybe I'm losing my mind. But before the thought had even completed itself, the small piece of wood in his pocket seemed to throb and heat.

Blowing out a sigh, he closed his eyes, running his fingers

through his tumbled blond hair. "Okay. Find Tom. I want him back starting Monday, if he is willing, with a ten percent pay increase."

"Tuh . . . ten percent?" she repeated faintly.

"Yes," he called over his shoulder as he jogged down the stairs. "Don't worry. You're getting fifteen."

He heard an odd muffled thud, but didn't look back. If he had, he would have seen his ever graceful butler sitting flat on her butt in the middle of the landing.

"Choices," he muttered to himself as he slid behind the wheel of his car. His hands flexed on the steering wheel and a wicked, boyish grin lit his face. Damn, he'd dreamed about having one of these, just getting out on the highway and opening it up. But he'd never done it—

"What a waste," he muttered, jamming the CLK into drive and speeding down the driveway. Damn, if it was summer, he could open the windows, feel the sun, the wind. Had that ever mattered?

No. Driving fast ate up gas, which ate up money. And why in the hell did that really matter? "Got more than I'll ever spend," he said quietly, his pale blue eyes soft as he admitted that to himself.

What fun was the money—if he didn't put it to good use?

He couldn't remember the last time he'd been to the mall. And he knew he hadn't ever come on Christmas Eve. He knew where it was, out on Shelbyville Road, but he didn't think he'd gone into a mall in more than five years.

"This place is a madhouse," he whispered to himself as he sat staring at the mall from the driver's seat.

Shaking his head, he grinned, a white flash of straight, even teeth in his face as he climbed out, slamming the door behind him. "Might as well dive right in," he said. Then he laughed. "I sound like a lunatic talking to myself."

As his long, lean legs ate up the distance, he plotted out his attack. He always worked better with a plan. The toy store was the most important, but he had to make sure there was a fine spread on the table for tomorrow. Maybe a new briefcase for Daniel, with a big fat check inside . . . and a letter begging him to come back. The check could be incentive, a signing bonus, of sorts, for coming back.

Daniel might accept that.

On the way out of the mall, with the assistance of a wide-eyed teenage girl helping to carry the bags, he saw a store set up in a trailer just outside. The rich smell of smoking meat carried to him on the wind as he recognized the name of the small catering place.

Perfect . . .

It took several hundred dollars, but he convinced the manager of the store that he really needed that ham tomorrow. With a soft sigh, and a look heavenward, she offered, "I can have one ready tonight—it will take a while, but . . ."

"That would be wonderful," Eben said, grinning widely at her as he tucked the money into her hand. It was after he had driven away that she realized it was five hundred, not the three hundred he had initially bribed her with.

Now, he just needed somebody to play delivery boy. The stuff had to get to Daniel's house tonight, but Eben was a little leery about showing his face just yet. Tomorrow, he'd face Daniel.

Not tonight.

5

ara stretched her arms high overhead, looking out over the sea of bent heads, her heart wrenching as she heard a young giggle. In the corner, Mac McGowan was playing Santa to a small group of youngsters. The oldest was probably five. Much older than that, growing up the way these kids did, and the kids didn't want to go to a stranger. Even some of the young ones were leery of the man in red, but Mac won them over.

He'd been doing it for years, even with her. Sighing, she pressed a hand to her back, stiff and aching from spending so long on her feet. Why do you keep coming here, Cara? she asked herself.

This same shelter, every Christmas, for more than five years.

Sixteen years ago—she'd been twelve—was the last year

she had spent having to eat at one of these tables. The year her mother died, leaving her with nobody and nothing in the world. Not that she'd ever had much even with her mom. They'd lived on the streets more often than not, after her mom had taken Cara in the middle of the night, running away from an abusive husband.

They'd eaten in shelters, lived in the old run-down car . . . stolen food. Then her mom had died and Cara was alone, and she'd never tried to beg for food. Her mom had warned her, a kid alone would get taken by the state. So she stole, and she crept into the shelter with larger groups of people, hiding among their numbers. And for a while, she'd gotten by.

Mac was the one who had finally called Social Services, and she had been taken, kicking and screaming, to foster care.

It had saved her life, made her life. And it had only taken ten years for her to find her way back here to look Mac in the eye and tell him thank you. He had smiled, that sweet smile she remembered, only now in an older, wearier face.

Her parents, the people who had taken her in and later adopted her, had been dead for three years, from a car wreck driving home from vacation. But before that, they'd spent two Christmas Eves here with her, serving up the simple, hot food to the people who wandered in through the doors.

Her dad had collected money at his workplace and bought presents for the kids. Simple toys, dolls and cars, things easily tucked into a pocket. And Cara and her mother had led cloth-ing drives to collect enough decent coats.

She really needed to be able to walk away from this, though.

It was breaking her heart, looking at the small children, the mothers with weary, hopeless eyes, so lost and broken. And Cara could do nothing.

Her lashes dropped and she sighed.

Nothing, because there wasn't enough money to do what needed to be done.

Money. The root of all evil, so it was said, and that had to be true. How else could something so trivial stand in the way of helping people? Wasn't that the most important thing?

People, and not numbers stamped on paper.

Money . . .

As Eben slowed to a stop, he tried to figure out exactly why he was stopping. Why he had taken that exit, one that had led him clear into Louisville's west side. Geez, he never came down here. He wouldn't be able to tell north from south down here.

So why in the hell was he standing in front of an old church? Why did he feel like this was where he needed to be?

"You're losing your mind, Eben," he muttered, running a hand through his hair as he climbed out of the car, frowning as he glanced around. I'm nuts, leaving my car in a place like this . . . It's not even going to be here when I get back.

He stepped through the door, assaulted by the smell of unwashed bodies, filth . . . and despair. Eben didn't realize such a human emotion could be recognized just by breathing in the air.

As he looked around, he saw tired women, some of them with battered faces, all of them with a weary, resigned look in their eyes. Older people, gray-haired grannies who should be at home in rocking chairs, men sitting on the floor, dog tags around their necks, their eyes dark, haunted.

And kids. Damn . . . the kids . . . so many of them.

And it was from the kids that he realized there was more than just despair in the air.

There was also life, and hope. Laughter coming from some of those kids as they crowded around a Santa who laughed and chuckled as he watched the sparkling, dancing eyes of the children. There was the smell of hot, simple, nourishing food, and . . . pine.

Pine trees . . . With a small grin, he studied the massive tree in one corner of the large rec room, his eyes roaming over the twinkling lights and the decorations, many handmade, most likely by the kids at Santa's feet. Boughs of pine draped from the exposed rafters, intertwined with sparkling white lights.

Damn, it had been years since he had seen a real Christmas tree, one obviously decorated by those meant to enjoy it. And he'd forgotten how much pleasure just looking at a Christmas tree could give him. That had been . . . years ago, not since he had been a teenager.

A low, husky laugh drifted to him through the cacophony of sound. How he heard it, much less recognized it, made no sense. But as his head whipped around, he knew who he'd see.

He also knew, with a bone-deep certainty, exactly why he was here.

It was for her.

That smile of hers—seductively sweet and wicked all at the same time—had haunted him for months, until he'd forced himself to simply stop thinking of her. It had taken all of his willpower to do it, all of his focus to think of something, somebody other than her.

She had intruded upon his mind at the oddest of times, so he had done what he had thought was best and forced her out of his thoughts.

What would have been best would have been to seek her out, beg her forgiveness for the way he had treated her . . . and try to forge some sort of relationship with her.

And that was why he had been drawn here tonight.

Choices . . .

Drawing the small carving from his pocket, he rubbed it with his thumb. He had made the wrong one so often now that it seemed that was all he knew how to do. Maybe that was why it was so hard to take a slow step in her direction . . . and then another, followed by another . . .

Cara felt the intense gaze on her neck as she held out the plate to the bent old man in front of her. He had fought in the Vietnam War, she knew, from past conversations with him. His fiancée had left him while he was gone, clinging to the peace movement of the sixties.

He had come back, hurting inside, but looking for the girl he had loved all of his life, thinking everything would be okay . . . but it hadn't been.

After that, somewhere along the way, he had simply given

up—and now he was here, smiling that sweet smile at her before he made his way over to a table and dug into the food with hands that shook.

Scanning the tables, she searched for the source of those watchful eyes, but saw only people eating their food, kids with proud smiles showing their small prizes to their grim-eyed mamas. She frowned and shrugged, turning her head to check on Mr. McGowan. He was getting older—it was in the tired way he moved, the occasional tightening of his face as his body pained him.

But right now, he was having the time of his life. With a smile, she looked back to the line, reaching for the ladle . . . and then she froze.

Slowly, Cara turned her gaze back to the entryway of the church's rec hall.

Eben . . . she mouthed, her heart tightening in her chest.

He was staring at her with intent, watchful eyes. As she met his stare, a rare, solemn smile edged up the corners of his mouth. She swallowed and turned her eyes back to the lady in line, staring at her in bemusement.

Behind her, Cally Anders chuckled. "He been staring at you like that since he walked through the door five minutes ago, girl," the older woman drawled, grinning as she reached around and took the soup ladle from Cara. "Go on, already."

"He's not here to see me," she said faintly. Even though she had dreamed for months that he'd come after her . . . somehow, in the few short months she'd worked with him on a takeover project, she had fallen in love with him, and that one wild night together had only intensified her feelings.

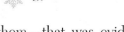

However, Eben didn't return them—that was evident in how easily he'd walked away, how he'd transferred her out of his department, how he'd ignored her for three years.

But Cara took off her apron and tossed it on a table, walking out from behind the counter, her eyes held by his. Something about that intense stare had her heart pounding, her mouth going dry. Curling her hands into loose fists, she jammed them into the pockets of the brightly colored Christmas cardigan she had pulled on with her jeans.

Coming to a stop before him, Cara forced her lips into a casual smile. "What brings you to Bethel, Mr. Marley? You lost?"

A different light entered his eyes. "I was. I'm not now, but thank you," he said quietly in that polite, cultured voice.

She pondered that for a moment, her mouth pursed as she studied him. "Okay . . . I give up, Mr. Marley," she said, shaking her head. "What are you doing here?"

Her breath locked in her chest as he took a minuscule step forward, lowering his head to whisper softly, "I realize I didn't conduct myself in the best manner, but don't you think you know me well enough to call me Eben? You did then."

Blood stained her cheeks bright red as he lifted his head and met her gaze. "Ahhh . . . That night was an anomaly—didn't change anything, remember?"

"Oh, I remember that night," he said obliquely. "All too well." He looked away, studying the people around him with unreadable eyes. "What brings you here?"

Touching her tongue to her lower lip, she wondered what

he'd say if he knew her real reasons. She hedged, shrugging casually as she said, "My parents and I helped out here for a few years. They died three years ago, but I keep coming."

"I'm sorry," he said, sliding his pale blue gaze back to her, an odd light in it. He looked almost—sympathetic. But she hadn't thought sympathy was an emotion Eben Marley could feel.

Her throat tightened. With a silent nod, she acknowledged his words. Long moments passed before she forced herself to speak. "You never did say why you were here . . . Eben."

His gaze swung back to her; his lids drooped low over those indescribable blue eyes. It fell to her lips for a long moment before he met her stare again. "Would you believe me if I said I didn't know what I was doing here?"

Not a lie, really. Until he had seen her dark head bent over the counter, he hadn't known what he was doing here.

She nibbled on her lower lip with small, white teeth, her eyes narrowing as she scrutinized him. He had half expected a slap in the face from her, but she didn't seem upset to see him . . . he could even feel how un-upset she was. See it in the way her lashes dropped to shield those pretty green eyes from him. In the way her breathing had picked up as he lowered his mouth to murmur in her ear.

The scent of her flooded his head, and he was half drunk on it.

Spreading his hands wide, he said, "I've never been here in my life, never even heard of it—I was driving through Louis-ville and just had this . . . urge, I guess you'd call it."

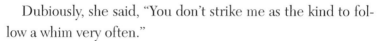

Dubiously, she said, "You don't strike me as the kind to follow a whim very often."

He wasn't. She had been one of his rare ones, a sudden, driving need to feel her beneath him, to feel just how hot and tight her pussy would be as he went down on her. Most of the women he slept with were ones he had seduced, with the only goal from the get-go being to ease the driving need to fuck.

She had been different, though, watching him with those wide eyes, trying to hide her attraction for him, never once approaching him . . . until that night. He didn't like being approached; he wanted to scope out what he wanted, move in and take, plain and simple. Any time a woman tried it the other way, she got shot down.

Not Cara though.

Lifting one shoulder in a shrug, he said thoughtfully, "I've been thinking that I need to listen to those little urges more often." Then he focused his gaze back on the patrons of the shelter. "Can I help?"

The laugh that bubbled out of her throat had him lifting a brow at her. She muffled the giggle, falling into silence as she looked at him. "You want to help . . . here."

A frown tugged at his lips as he studied the people there, his heart tugging as he looked at one shy little girl who kept staring at Santa with yearning eyes. But every time her mama urged her to go, she would bury her face, clinging for dear life. "I don't necessarily think want is the correct term. But I need to," he said finally.

A dull sense of shame rushed through him as she cocked her head at him. "Are you feeling okay, Eben? You're not acting like yourself."

He laughed, a dry, humorless sound. "I don't think I've ever felt better, if you want the truth. And I've never acted less like myself in my life."

So she showed him the ropes, all the while sliding him odd little glances that she thought he didn't see. He ended up in her place, behind the counter, serving people hot, homemade soup that smelled better than anything had in quite a while.

Well, besides Cara.

The simple potato soup smelled like ambrosia, and Eben tried to recall the last time he'd had something as simple as homemade potato soup. Too long, he decided a few hours later as he dug into the bowl somebody had urged into his hands.

Cara was out mingling with people, talking to the women and the older folks, cuddling babies, a smile on her lovely face. And although she tried desperately to hide it, he saw the echoes of grief in her eyes.

She didn't want to be here.

He waited until the last person had been served, the last present given from Santa, before he approached her. The people were slowly drifting out, one by one, and Cara was bent over a table, gathering up bowls and plates, a forlorn look in her eyes.

"If being here bothers you so much, how come you're here?" he asked, straddling a bench as she walked by, reaching out and laying a hand on her arm.

Cara stilled, her eyes dark in her pale face. For a long moment, she was silent, staring into the distance, seeing nothing.

Finally, she lifted her gaze to him, shrugging halfheartedly.

"Would you believe I have to be here?" she asked, echoing his question from earlier. "Not everybody has a warm home, a loving family. I have to do what I can to make it a little better for them."

He cocked a brow at her, his heart tugging as the lost look he had glimpsed on her face throughout the night resurfaced. "It seems to me to be a little more than that," he said quietly.

Cara's eyes narrowed and he felt the chill emanating from her so strongly that he wished he'd kept his mouth shut. "Hmm . . . you think you know me well enough to make that sort of statement, Eben?" she asked, her voice brittle.

He blanked his face, rising slowly. With a single nod, he said, "You've got a point. I never took the chance to get to know you, did I?" He forced a smile for her and said quietly, "Have a Merry Christmas, Cara."

He felt her eyes on him the entire way to the door, where he retrieved his coat from the coat rack. Without looking back, he walked out the door.

And what a pleasant surprise—his car was still there. And it even appeared to be in one piece.

Cara could have kicked herself. "Damn it, how stupid are you going to get, Cara?" she muttered to herself, heading to the door seconds after it swung closed behind him.

He was just ducking low to climb into his car as she shoved the door open. As he caught sight of her, that straight blond brow lifting as he met her gaze, Cara felt her heart tremble.

There was something in his eyes she hadn't ever seen there before.

Humanity, she supposed. An empathy and understanding she suspected was very foreign to him.

She also suspected that her last remark had cut him. Cara couldn't help but feel a little pleased over that. After all, he had snubbed her pretty badly a few years ago. Crossing her sweater-covered arms over her chest, she walked up to him, studying his face.

He closed the door, propping his elbows on the roof of the car as he looked at her. "It's cold outside, Cara. Go back inside."

"Why are you here, Eben?"

A slow smile spread across his face as he shrugged. "You wouldn't believe me if I told you," he said, lifting his face to the dark, winter sky.

"Try me," she offered, shivering in her sweater as the wind whipped down the cold streets. What was going on here? she wondered.

He came from around the car, shrugging out of his coat. She closed her eyes in bliss as he wrapped her in it, the warmth seeping into her bones, his scent covering her. Her nipples peaked and stiffened as he ran the back of his knuckles down her cheek.

His eyes . . . Damn, she could get lost in his eyes. They had always been mesmerizing, that pale, ice-blue gaze. But today had been the first time she had ever seen warmth in them.

Not sexual heat, that was different . . . but warmth. Something so simple, so human . . . and very unlike him.

His other hand came up and he cupped her face, staring

down at her intently as he lowered his head, stopping when his mouth was just a whisper away from hers. "You . . ." he murmured just before he slanted his mouth across hers.

The taste of him exploded through her, a gasp falling from her as she arched up against him. He stroked his tongue teasingly over hers as his hands slid down from her face to wrap around her waist, drawing her against him. Her nipples burned inside the silk of her bra, throbbing and aching. One long-fingered hand slid down to cup her ass, bringing her firmly against him.

Cream drenched her panties, and just like that, she was ready for him. He could have urged her into the backseat of his car and she would have gone willingly. Against the soft curve of her belly, she felt his sex throb—the feel of him against her made her pussy ache.

She started to whimper and moan, deep and low in her throat, as he pumped his hips against her belly. A growl rumbled out of him as he pulled his mouth away from hers. His free hand slid up and fisted in her short cap of hair, pulling her head back and to the side, exposing her neck to the sharp, hungry press of his teeth.

"Your taste—I've never forgotten," he rasped.

Shivering, she lifted her lashes as he sighed roughly, pulling away from her just a fraction. Unwittingly, her tongue slid out, capturing his taste on her lips. Her lashes fluttered closed as she savored it.

Forcing a breath into her lungs, she opened her eyes, watching him as she lifted her hand and pressed her index finger against his lip. "I never forgot yours," she replied in a husky whisper.

The pounding of her heart seemed to roar in her ears as he opened his mouth and bit down lightly on the tip of her finger, stroking it lightly with his tongue.

But his next move simply left her floundering. He released his grip on her finger and drew her up against him, one hand cupping the back of her neck, the other arm wrapped firmly around her waist, holding her snug against him. Slowly, she wrapped her arms around his torso, stroking the long, powerful lines of his back with one hand, wondering yet again . . . What is going on?

"I had you reassigned because I didn't like how often you kept creeping into my thoughts," he whispered gruffly. "Nobody has ever lingered in my mind for more than a day—until you."

He moved away then, pacing over to the curb, his shoulders stiff with tension as he stared into the night.

"Eben—"

He whirled around, his eyes hot on her face. "You stayed with me, even after that, do you know that? Your face would slide into my dreams at night, when I didn't have any control. I fantasized—very briefly—about convincing you into some sort of . . . arrangement, if you would . . . Anything so I could see your eyes go black as you started to come," he murmured.

Her eyes flashed with indignation as he moved in on her, his hand coming up to cup her chin. "I wanted you, but I wouldn't have whored for you," she said coolly, her eyes narrowing to slits.

"Hmmm . . . Maybe that's why I never asked," he said, quirking a brow at her. "Or maybe it's because I was worried

I'd do quite a bit to convince you to come to me. Your face haunts me . . ."

Her heart rolled over in her chest as he repeated himself, shaking his head as though he didn't understand it.

He lowered his lips to brush gently against hers and then he was gone. "Go back inside, Cara," he said gruffly, striding over to his car and jerking the door open again.

His eyes lingered on her face until she did just that.

6

His hands were shaking as he drove away.

Eben gripped the steering wheel as though it were the only thing anchoring him. Damn it, she was still as sweet now as she had been then. He'd held her in his arms, kissed that sulky mouth, spread her thighs and lifted her ass in his hands, plunged his tongue deep inside the well of her slick, snug pussy, and watched the glory of a climax break over her.

Then he'd walked away from her, pushed her away—of all the foolish things he had done, Eben was certain that this had to be one of the worst. How could he have given that up? How had he thought he didn't need just that in his life?

"Well, boy, before now, you didn't realize just how necessary that was."

"Damn it!" Eben bellowed as his father wavered into view in the seat beside him. His foot slammed down on the brake as he cut his eyes to the right and stared at the image of his dead father.

In a hollow, echoing voice, Taylor said with a grin, "Ebenezer Marley, I swear, you look like you've seen a ghost!"

"Damn it, Dad, are you trying to give me a heart attack?" he demanded.

Taylor chuckled. "No need to worry about that—not now. You finally figured out what you needed to know, and I think you're going to be fine," the older Marley said, smiling fondly at his son. "I'm sorry, son. This is my fault, in part. I never raised you to believe there was anything other than the job and the money. By the time I understood that myself, you were already walking down your own road."

Eben scowled to hide the swell of emotion inside him. "I made my own choices, Dad. For a very long time. You aren't to blame."

Taylor sighed, lifting one shoulder in a shrug. "That's the job of a parent, Eben. Listen, don't forget what you've learned today . . . and go get that girl."

His words were still echoing in the car, but Taylor Marley was gone.

And Eben had a gut-deep feeling that it was for good this time. He wouldn't be seeing his father again . . . on this side of life.

With a tight throat and stinging eyes, Eben let off the brake and started back down the silent street.

✿   ✿   ✿

It was a long drive from West Louisville to the posh area out-side of town where Eben lived. Cara hadn't exactly figured out what she was doing. What if he threw her out? What if he laughed at her?

What if he wasn't home?

Or what if he was . . . and he was with another woman?

A soft voice inside her heart whispered that wasn't going to happen. Eben had stared at her in a way no man had ever looked at her before—like she was the center of his universe.

When she finally reached his house, it was late, very late, nearly midnight. She lifted her eyes to the dark sky, staring at the stars that hung like diamonds in the air. Her breath es-caped her in a puffy cloud as she tried once more to quell the nerves in her belly.

This was so not like her.

But he had been acting so—not like Eben.

He seemed more approachable, more alive. And his hands, his mouth . . . He had clung to her like she was the only thing in his world. Even that one night together years earlier, there had been a part of him that was disconnected, unmoved by everything—and he had loved her in an almost clinical, focused manner, as though he was determined to make her scream X amount of times, as though he was measuring each response.

Earlier, when he had kissed her, she had been the only thing in his world.

Something told her that was very, very unusual for him. And it was that quiet little urging voice that she was listening to right now. She planned to blame that little voice if she got tossed out on her butt.

The long, paved road wove around Eben's estate. It had been four years since she'd been here, at a business dinner meeting, working with her new boss, meeting Eben for the first time.

And it was as amazing now as it was then, the windows, and there seemed to be a thousand of them, all sparkling under the light of the full moon. The moon hung low and fat in the air, casting its silvery light all over the sumptuous estate. There were more lights blazing, even though it was later now than it had been then.

So he was awake, she figured, nibbling nervously on her lower lip as she slowly walked up the ornate walkway. Egads . . . even the sidewalks are fancy, she thought as she glanced down. She'd been too much in awe of the house to notice anything else when she had come here that one and only time.

Pressing a finger to the doorbell, she took a deep breath, trying to compose herself. Hell, maybe the butler would turn her away—she never doubted there'd be a butler there. Even if it was past eleven o'clock on Christmas Eve.

So when Eben himself opened the door, bare-chested, his pale blond hair tousled, she was at a loss for words.

Except for . . . Damn, he's hot . . .

Unconsciously, her tongue slid out to wet her lips as her eyes drifted down the hard, sculpted wall of his chest.

Finally, she tore her eyes away from those six-pack abs and lifted her gaze to find him watching her with an arched brow, a bemused, questioning smile on his face. Her eyes rested briefly on that mouth, one corner canted up, the hint of a dimple in his cheek.

"Merry Christmas," she said finally, keeping her hands fisted in the pockets of the long, rich velvet cloak she'd pulled on. One of her few indulgences, the sumptuous thing was made of real silk velvet, with that soft sheen only the best of velvets had. It lay against her naked body, the wind snaking in under the hem to nip at her bare legs.

He grinned a little wider as he said, "You've said that once already, today, haven't you?"

She shrugged and the edges of the cloak shifted just enough—she watched as his eyes cut to the front of the cloak for the quickest of seconds, hot and intent. When he looked back into her eyes, it was with a bland gaze. But she'd seen the flames.

"Maybe, but I didn't give you a present," she said huskily.

He frowned, brows dropping low over his eyes. "You don't need to give—"

Interrupting, she asked, "Don't you want to know what it is?" And with a naughty little smile, she reached up and flipped open the heavy pewter clasp, shrugging her shoulders so that the velvet fell away. She caught the heavy length in her hand and just stood there, waiting, as he stared at her scantily covered body with hot, hungry eyes. The red push-up bra gleamed against the pale ivory of her skin, the temporary tattoo she'd applied the day before rested right above the line of the skirted garter belt she wore.

Skinny little garters held up the opaque black stockings, and she wore the high-heeled, red fuck-me shoes she had bought on a whim a few weeks earlier.

His voice shook slightly as he rasped, "I don't think I've

been good enough for that kind of present." Then he grimaced. "Unless you just plan on letting me look before you walk away."

The cold rippled down her skin and she shivered, but kept her arms hanging loose at her sides. With a slight smile, she said, "I wasn't planning on doing that."

Her breath left her in a rush as he grabbed her and jerked her against him, whirling around as he kicked the door shut. Before she could so much as gasp for a breath of air, he had his mouth slanted demandingly across hers, his tongue driving deep inside as his hands palmed her ass.

Moaning in delight, she wrapped her arms around his neck and tangled her tongue with his. Her nipples stabbed into the silk of her bra, hot and tight and burning. Pussy wet and aching, she rocked her hips against his pelvis, sobbing into his mouth as he lifted her and started to grind his covered cock against the thin silk of her thong.

"Damn it, you're so fucking wet and hot, I can feel you through my jeans," he groaned against her lips. He turned her around, leaning her back against the door as he pulled away.

Her body trembled, crying out at the loss of his heat, but she almost whimpered as he sank to his knees in front of her. "I shouldn't be doing this," he whispered. "I treated you like hell . . . I don't deserve to so much as even look at you."

Cara opened her lips to . . . do something, anything to keep him from pulling away, but before she could, he leaned forward and pressed his mouth against the silk that separated her pussy from his tongue. Agile fingers flipped open the garters and her breath caught again as he slid his hot hands under the short, formfitting, skirted garter belt. The heated, calloused flesh of his palms cupped her butt, lifting the silky, deep red fabric and baring the skinny swatch of silk that ran between her thighs.

He nuzzled her through the thong before he pulled it aside, leaving her sex bare. She heard him groan like a man offered a feast after a famine and then his hands were on her thighs, spreading them, reaching behind her knee to lift one leg and drape it over his shoulder.

His tongue, silken and fiery hot, stabbed at her clit, working it with teeth and tongue as he started to push two fingers deep inside her. She felt that hungry growl that rose from him in a vibrating caress of breath that left her dazed with an embarrassed sort of pleasure.

She could make this arrogant, cool man into a hungry, ravenous being of need and desire . . . Her.

A soft, hoarse keen fell from her lips as he shifted position and started to fuck his tongue in and out of her weeping cleft. Her belly tensed, and her nipples tightened painfully as he worked her closer to that bright, shimmering edge of climax.

Wet, hungry noises filled the air as he drank her cream down and lapped and suckled at her flesh. A fist of sensation shot through her time after time with each silken lash of his tongue, until she was rocking her hips against his face, her hands fisting in his hair, riding the waves of pleasure as she started to come.

Cara felt her legs buckling beneath her and she didn't care, barely even realized that he supported her weight as she fell, screaming out his name, her voice rough and hoarse.

As the shudders continued to course through her body, she started to float down to earth, the world actually moving around her . . . and then she realized that she was moving, not the world, as he guided her down, the silk of her cloak between the hard floor and her back.

Her lids fluttered closed and she just hummed under her breath with pleasure. His hands ran up the length of her thighs, beneath the snug-fitting garter belt, hooked over the waistband of her thong and slid it down.

And she just . . . floated.

His hands shaking, Eben tore open the fly of his jeans before he levered his body over hers. "Open your eyes," he demanded gruffly, staring down at her flushed face, a sated, smug smile curving her lips. As the heavy fringe of her lashes lifted, he wedged his hips between the soft, satiny skin of her thighs, brushing against her entrance with the head of his cock.

The satiny heat tempted him and he groaned, pushing more heavily against her, shuddering at the contact as the head of his cock breached the dew-slickened lips of her pussy, sliding just barely inside.

Damn it, he hadn't fucked a woman without a rubber in years, not since . . . Her name escaped him, a woman he'd been certain he'd never forget, but as he stared into Cara's flushed face, at her desire-clouded green eyes, he couldn't think of anything beyond her.

"Rubber," he gritted out, trying to remind himself.

Under him, she hummed, sliding her hands down over his ribs, cupping them around his hips and whispering, "No . . . just you . . . just me . . ."

Swearing shakily, he tried to remind himself of all the reasons that wasn't a good idea . . . but couldn't think of a single one, not when she lifted her hips, forcing an aching inch of his cock inside. Not when she dug her nails into the taut skin of his ass and pulled him against her. With a hoarse whisper, he sank home, feeling the satiny wet heat of her pussy close tight and snug around him.

Rolling onto his back, he gripped her waist, rocking her back and forth, his breath left him in harsh ragged pants. She sat upright, driving her weight further down on him, her eyes fluttering wide, a startled little gasp escaping her. Then a smug little feline smile curved her lips and she started to ride, sliding her hands up her torso, over her breasts, before she laced her fingers behind her head, her lashes drifting down.

Eben had never seen a sight so lovely, so erotic, in his life. His heart squeezed in his chest, then seemed to expand as he arched his hips up, pushing harder and harder into her silken sheath, his cock pounding, throbbing—harder than he had ever been in his life. A soft sob escaped her and she braced her hands on his chest, leaning forward and lifting her weight. He growled softly as she pulled up, and he gripped her hips, certain she was going to pull away, but all she did was drop her weight back down on him, taking his cock inside in one fast, deep stroke. Then she lifted, dropped back down, taking him inside her pussy again, and again . . . faster and faster.

Staring up at her, his eyes locked on her face, he watched as she ran her tongue over her lips, a soft purr falling from her mouth. He stared at her hands as she slid them over her torso, up to cup her breasts, then on up until she could run her fingers through her hair, her eyes slitted and glittering in the dim light of the foyer.

The muscles in her belly worked as she rocked against him. As he moved his gaze downward, he could see the slick, wet flesh of his cock as it disappeared back inside her snug sheath. He watched for a long moment as she rode him, so sweetly, so fucking seductively that he thought he'd climax with every damned stroke.

Gritting his teeth, Eben fought not to come, to stay just there as she continued that slow, steady rhythm. His balls drew tight, his fingers dug into her hips, his teeth clenched, a spasm of agonized pleasure jolting through him. Fucking her, especially like this, skin to skin, was like trying to fuck a lightning bolt, and he didn't know if he could survive a pleasure this hot, this intense and all-consuming. The cream-slicked tissues of her pussy were fiery hot, tight, flexing around his cock with each breath she took.

"Damn, you're going to kill me, Cara," he gasped out as she lifted again, slower this time, teasingly.

Dimly, part of him saw the shocked pleasure roll over her face, but he didn't comprehend it as he started to arch into her teasing strokes, his fingers biting into her flesh as he forced her back into a hard, fast rhythm. She gasped out his name, and her pussy clenched around him with a viselike grip, the creamy, wet heat of that embrace so tight, so snug. With a savage growl, he rolled, taking her under him, and plunged into her depths as his head swooped down and he took her mouth roughly. Her back arched, driving her tightly beaded nipples into his chest—hot, aching little points of sensation everywhere her skin touched him.

Feeding at her mouth, he fucked his cock in and out of her hot, wet little hole, growling in animalistic pleasure as jolt after jolt of sensation raced down his spine until he couldn't take anymore. The climax grabbed him by the throat, by the balls . . . by his heart as she sobbed his name. The bite of her fingers into his skin, the feel of her coming around him triggered his own climax. Eben erupted inside her just as she tore her lips away from his and screamed out, "Eben!" as she climaxed around him with almost vicious intensity.

On and on, his seed jetted into her depths, the milking sensations of her swollen pussy drawing it on forever. With a shaking sigh, as she finally spent him, he lowered himself onto her body, sliding down until his head was pillowed between the smooth globes of her heaving breasts.

"Best present I've ever gotten," he whispered, sliding one hand up until he could link it with hers.

7

Cara felt her heart contract almost painfully as he lifted his head and stared down at her through misty, almost dazed eyes. "Stay with me?" he asked, and he lifted her hand to his lips, pressing a kiss to it and watching her over their joined hands.

Stay . . . He wanted her to stay . . . Now that was the best present she'd ever gotten.

Because something told her Eben didn't invite women into his house, especially not for this, and never to stay, even for just a night.

She lifted up onto her elbow and pressed her lips to his mouth, whispering softly, "Yes, I think I'd love to."

A startled giggle left her as moments later he stood and swept her into his arms, Rhett Butler–style, carrying her up the staircase, his eyes intent on her face. A dreamy smile curved her lips, as the strength of that act touched something female deep inside of her.

After all, how many women have dreamt of being swept up and carried away, just like this?

Cara definitely had, and so many of her fantasies had been centered on Eben, since the first time she had met him. But she'd never expected it to happen, although she knew exactly how powerful a body he hid under those power suits of his.

Resting her head on his shoulder, she closed her eyes and reveled in the moment, barely blinking as he laid her down on a plush, heavenly bed, the mattress molding to her body like a hug.

"Open your eyes again, let me see you," he whispered gruffly, the mattress shifting just slightly as he lowered himself down beside her.

She lifted her lashes and stared at him, bemused, as he stared back at her as though she was the focus of his entire life. He lowered his head, brushing his lips down the slope of her breast, his breath caressing her flesh, tightening her nipples once more into aching buds. "I really think I'd like to keep you," he murmured, his tongue darting out to wrap briefly around her nipple.

His eyes gleamed like blue fire in the dim light of the room as he lifted his head to stare down at her. "Usually if there's something I want, I just offer up enough money—but I don't think that will work with you. I don't want that to work with you," he whispered, and there was that odd, bemused look on his face, in his eyes, as he gazed into her eyes. "But what will work? I totally failed the last time there was a woman who mattered to me, and I don't think she made me feel what you do. I couldn't make her happy, couldn't keep her . . . So what do I do to ensure that I'll make you happy? That you'll want to stay?"

Her lips curved into a tremulous smile, and tears stung her eyes as she cupped his face in her hands. "Maybe you should just try asking . . . later," she whispered, her voice husky and rough with emotion. "I want to savor every last second of this . . . and I want you to be sure."

His lashes drooped, hooding his eyes. A slight smile curved his lips and he murmured, "Well, at least that's a chance."

For her, there was little choice. Her heart was already his, she knew. She just wasn't so sure she wanted him knowing that until she was more certain of him—thus, the need to take it slowly. Rising, she pressed her lips to his, pushing lightly on his shoulders until he rolled onto his back.

As he rolled, she held still, breaking the contact with his lips, her eyes running over the firm, lean muscles of his body. A guy who seemed to spend all of his time in power suits really shouldn't look that good. Lightly, she traced the pads of her fingers over his pecs, sweeping down to stroke his hard belly before she moved lower, cupping her hand around the fullness of his erection. Feeling the hard, steely length jerk in her hand, she lowered her head and pressed a soft kiss to the tip.

Watching him from under the veil of her lashes, she took the crown of his cock into her mouth, rubbing it with her tongue as she moved her head in a slow, steady rhythm, licking away the come and cream that had dried on his cock. Humming under her breath in appreciation, she took him farther inside her mouth, until her lips were spread tight around his width and the head of his cock was bumping against the back of her throat.

His hands buried in the short strands of her hair as he started to rise against her, his eyes intent on her face, his jaw locked, a tic pulsing in his cheek. Pulling away, she flashed him a cheeky grin and asked, "Like what you see?"

"Hell, yes," he growled, using his grip on her hair to tug her back down.

As she took him back inside, she felt him shudder, and she couldn't help the internal smile that spread through her, that rush of feminine pride. With her hand wrapped around the base of his cock, she sucked on him, pulling away to teasingly lap at the clear drops of fluid that seeped from him. Lowering her head between his thighs she caught a patch of sensitive skin in her mouth, drawing on his sac and listening as he blistered the walls with a rough curse.

Cara grinned at him mischievously as she lowered her head, taking his cock inside her mouth, deeper and deeper, until the rounded head of his sex butted against the back of her throat.

In a blur of motion, he spilled her onto her back, staring down at her with a stark look of hunger on that poetically handsome face. With his knee, he pushed her thighs apart, driving inside her with one hard, deep thrust, his teeth bared, head thrown back so that the cords in his neck stood out.

With harsh, short digs of his hips, he sank inside her, quick, almost brutal thrusts that sent her shooting straight to the top as a sudden harsh orgasm ripped through her. Sobbing out his name, she locked her legs around his hips, pumping her pelvis in time with his deep, powerful thrusts, the muscles in her pussy gripping at his cock.

He slanted his mouth across hers, stealing her breath away as he plunged his tongue deep inside her mouth. One hand came up, plumping her breast, pinching and rolling the nipple between his fingers. Each pluck from his fingers arrowed down through her belly, tightening inside her womb.

Then hot, brilliant lights exploded in front of her eyes as his hand left her breast, stroking down her side to cup her ass, his fingers straying to caress the tight pucker of her ass. She screamed into his mouth as he pushed against the tight rosette, a forbidden, naughty pleasure she had dreamed about for years. Like a geyser, she came, cream pouring from deep inside her to coat his cock, his balls, and her thighs.

Eben gritted his teeth against the silken spasms in her pussy, the caresses driving him insane, until he couldn't take any more and flooded her hot little pussy. As she said his name again, this time in a soft, dazed whisper, he collapsed atop her and rolled to the side.

Slowly, they drifted to sleep, wrapped around each other.

Cara woke and stared at the elaborate canopy over her head, trying to figure out where she was. It wasn't a sensation she was unused to, not after so many years of living on the streets and then bouncing through foster home after foster home. But it had been years since she had woken up in some place other than her own bed—three years to be precise.

That one night with Eben . . .

Eben! Her eyes widened and she sat up, her gaze flying across the room.

As she encountered Eben's thoughtful blue gaze, she flushed, her heart starting to slam against her ribs.

"Hi," she whispered, uncertain of what to expect.

A soft smile canted up one corner of his mouth and he said, just as quietly, "Hi. Sleep well?"

Nodding, she tucked the sheet around her breasts. "Wonderfully, thanks."

Eben rose from the chair he had been lounging in and climbed on the bed, crawling across the lake-size width of it until he could kneel by her side. Her eyes locked on his face, nerves battling with the lust that was brewing in her belly. Her breath caught as he reached up and laced the fingers of one hand through her short cap of hair, angling her face up.

"I . . . I uh, I haven't brushed my teeth," she muttered, turning her head aside.

He laughed and caught her chin with his other hand as he lowered his head and slanted his mouth across hers. "I don't care," he rasped, rubbing his lips against hers, teasing, then deepening the kiss, plunging his tongue hungrily inside her mouth. Cara whimpered, reaching up to curl her hand around his wrist.

He pulled away, his eyes hot and hungry on her face, trailing one hand from her chin, stroking his finger down the long line of her neck.

And her belly rumbled.

Her eyes widened and blood rushed to her cheeks, an embarrassed laugh escaping her. He chuckled, sitting back on his heels, his eyes glinting as he said, "I guess you're hungry."

Sinking her teeth into her lip, she shifted and nodded. "I can wait a while though. I can eat when I get home," she murmured.

A golden brow cocked and he shrugged. "You could do that, I guess . . . although I was kind of hoping you'd eat here. Unless you have plans for Christmas Day."

"Christmas! Geez, I forgot," she said, laughing and running a hand through her hair. A sad smile curved her lips and she shrugged. "My parents died a few years ago—I didn't have any other family, so it's just me. I was invited to dinner tonight at a friend's, but . . ."

"I've got some things I need to do today," he said, his eyes moving past her to stare at the wall thoughtfully. "Important, and I have to do it alone . . . but I'd love it if you stayed for a while. Breakfast, at least."

Grinning, she said, "I'd love to."

Of course, she hadn't been expecting him to cook. But he did, and he did a damned good job, she decided as she dug into a Mexican-style omelet with gusto. "A man who can cook—a woman's dream," she teased.

Eben smiled, shrugging absently as he sat down across from her. "My mom died when I was young. It was just Dad and me. And he didn't cook very well." Grimacing, he added, "Until I was about ten or eleven, I didn't realize you could do much with that shiny metal box in the kitchen—you know, the one that gets hot."

She grinned at him. "You've got a sense of humor, Eben. I never realized that."

He laughed at her, reaching to flick the long silver and black bead earrings that dangled from her ears. "I did a good job of hiding it," he replied. He took a bite of the eggs piled on his plate and shrugged. "Been a while since I've done much cooking, but not bad."

"Delicious," she corrected him, taking a heaping bite.

"You ought to try my steaks," he murmured, pushing the food around on his plate absently. A sigh escaped him and he set the fork down, leaning back in the chair, just watching her.

Under that intent scrutiny, she squirmed in her chair. "Aren't you hungry?"

A sensual smile curved his lips and he said in a low, husky voice, "Not for food."

Her cheeks heated and she licked her lips nervously before taking another bite. "Can I ask you something?" Keeping her eyes on her plate, she waited until he responded with a "yes" before she took a deep breath and blurted out the question that had been on the tip of her tongue ever since yesterday at the shelter.

"What's going on with you? You act so—different. Sort of the same, but at the same time, not the same at all." Then she sneaked a quick look at him, her nose wrinkling as she asked, "Does that make any sense?"

The look on his face, one of regret so strong it damn near brought tears to her eyes, made her wish she hadn't asked. After a long moment when she didn't think he was going to answer, he finally ran a hand through his hair and said quietly, "I had an . . . epiphany, of sorts. And I feel like I've been walking in the dark for most of my life, and somebody suddenly turned on the lights."

A thoughtful frown crossed her face. "Living in the dark how?"

Instead of explaining that, he said, "You know, a few months ago I fired my best man in the design department. He had taken more time off than I allow employees. He always had his work done, but still. And then I told him he needed to go out of town on some business trips that would take him away from home for a month at a time. He wouldn't go, so I fired him. You know Dan Wilson?" She heard him swallow, saw his eyes close as he folded his hands around his coffee mug. "He has a sick little girl . . . You know that?"

Cara whispered quietly, "Yes. Livvy. I've heard about her."

"What kind of bastard fires a guy, one with a family, just because he doesn't like the idea of going out of town for a month at a time?" he asked softly, his pale blue eyes bleak and cold. "He worked for me for ten years—I never knew a damned thing about him except that he had a sharp mind and he didn't cost me money."

Cara's heart wrenched at the emptiness she saw in his eyes.

He slid her a quick glance, his lips twisting in a self-deprecating smile. "Real class act you spent the night with, huh, Cara? Of course, you ought to know what kind of class act I am. After all, look at how I treated you."

It still stung, thinking of that night. But she was coming to understand that he had been scared, and had shoved her away because of that fear. That didn't make it right, but it did make it understandable. A little less painful. Silent, she reached for the exquisitely cut crystal glass of orange juice, drinking a little to wet her dry throat. To do something with her hands. As she tried to formulate something to say to him, he laughed, the sound dark and humorless.

"You can't think of anything to say to me, can you?"

Her eyes softened and she whispered, "Oh, Eben. You know, everybody does some things in life that they aren't proud of. They're not unforgivable—if you don't keep repeating them."

He snorted derisively. "You have no idea just how many things I've done that I'm not proud of, Cara. My list of sins is immeasurable."

Cara laughed. "Your worst sins, Eben, stem from being a little too selfish, a little too greedy . . . and just living with blinders on. There are much worse sins—killing, stealing from the people who provide for you, adultery, beating and abusing those you should have taken care of." Her throat went tight as long-suppressed memories tried to slip into her mind. "Nothing you've done is something that you can't move past."

"How can you be so sure? You don't even know the half of it," he muttered, pressing the pads of his fingers to his eyes.

He looks so weary, she thought. Sighing, she replied, "Because you want to move past it. If you want it enough, you will. The people in life who truly matter will see a different person, if that's what you want to be. A person can forgive a great deal, when it matters." Rising from her chair, she walked around the table, bending down and wrapping her arms around his neck and shoulders from behind. "You matter."

His hand came up, folding over hers. "You're amazing, Cara. You know that?"

She laughed. "Thank you—twenty-eight years of practice."

Craning his head around, he looked at her. "I thought you were twenty-six," he said, frowning. "You were twenty-four . . ."

His voice trailed away and a dull flush stained his cheeks. Cara giggled, leaning down and pressing a kiss to his cheek. "Yes . . . and I turned twenty-five a few months later, and that was three years ago. Today's my birthday, if you can believe that."

He arched a brow. "Happy birthday," he said softly. He shifted until he could reach around behind him and draw her into his lap. Cuddling against the warm wall of his chest, Cara listened to the steady sound of his heartbeat, smiling as he started to rub her back. "Don't you have something special to be doing for your birthday? A party? Family to visit?"

A sad smile curved her lips once more. "I don't put much into birthdays—I love the holiday season, the rush and wonder of it. But since my parents died . . . and my friends want to spend their day with their families. If they knew I was winging it alone, several of them would pitch a fit. But I'm used to it."

"You shouldn't be," he murmured.

Her heart flipped as he cupped her chin in his hand, lowering his mouth to kiss her gently. "Maybe I could take you to dinner tomorrow," he said softly, his voice hesitant.

"I'd like that," she said. Lowering her head back to his shoulder, she sighed as his arms folded around her. "So what exactly are you doing today? Can't be business, not on Christmas." Gently, she teased, "Not even you tried to make us work on Christmas Day."

He laughed dryly. "No. Just Christmas Eve, the day after Thanksgiving, the Fourth of July," he said sourly, but his eyes glinted at her. "It's sort of business—going to see Dan. See if he'll take his old job back . . ." A hint of a grin lit his tired face and he added, "I'm going to do something I've never done before. Play Santa Claus."

She laughed, squeezing his neck. "Sounds like fun. I love giving presents . . ."

8

ara smiled at him, waggling her fingers before
she shifted the car into reverse. Something inside
him felt hollow . . . damn it, he didn't want her leaving.

But she didn't need to see him eat crow, now did she?

Going to be hard enough to do it without an audience, he
thought grimly, shaking his head as he turned and headed
back inside the house. All he did was grab a coat and his
keys, knowing that if he stayed too long he'd talk himself out
of it.

Once on the road back into Louisville, Eben glanced at the
map, making sure he was heading in the right direction. He
had been assured that the presents had been delivered, along
with the food, by Michael, a bright-eyed, idealistic kid who
worked as a runner at Venture. Michael was one of the few

people who weren't swayed by Eben's grim demeanor, always laughing and inviting everybody to laugh with him.

It was just after eleven now, hopefully too early for lunch, but late enough that they had their morning to themselves.

As he slowed to a stop in front of the ramshackle old house, he blew out a breath. No time like the present.

It was so easy, he thought later, as he let Daniel talk him into a cup of coffee. Following him into a small, cramped office, Eben sat down on the single armchair that had been crammed into the room, along with the desk and chair in the corner.

So easy . . . Daniel had taken one long, slow look at him after he'd opened the door to Eben's knock. Just one look . . . and he had known where the presents had come from, where the food had come from. A slow smile had lit his face and he just shook his head before standing aside and letting Eben come slowly into the house.

"I learned long ago not to question a gift horse," Daniel said from the chair at the desk. "But I can't pretend I'm not curious as to what is going on, Mr. Marley."

Eben's eyes dropped to the briefcase at his feet, a smile lurking at his mouth. *Well, I had a visit from some ghosts, and they took me through A Christmas Carol and I've learned the error of my ways* . . . He laughed silently at the looks he'd receive if he told people that. They'd have him committed, no doubt. So he just stuck with the same line he'd given Cara.

"I had a revelation, that's all." He snagged the handle of the Italian leather briefcase, pushing it at Dan. "Here. This is for you. Before you open it, I want you to know that I would like you to come back to Venture. With a raise. And I'm getting the old insurance plan back. But regardless of your decision, the gift is yours to keep. And I don't want to hear anything else about it."

Daniel frowned thoughtfully as he ran his hands over the briefcase. "I enjoyed my job there. I hated being asked to leave. But I can't travel—"

"You won't have to. Travel for my employees is now strictly optional, with the exception of myself, the VPs, and a few other key people," Eben interrupted, shaking his head. "I'll be offering incentive pay to those who want to travel, but those who can't won't be penalized."

Daniel's brow arched. "Mr. Marley—"

"Eben," he corrected.

"Eben . . . I don't really understand what all this is about, but I'll be damned if I'm stupid enough to pass it up," Daniel said as he popped the latch on the briefcase.

The look on his face was almost comical, Eben thought, as Daniel reached inside with a shaky hand to pick up the check. "It's not certified. Usually I wouldn't give a check of that amount unless it was certified, but I couldn't get to the bank in time yesterday. But just let me know when you want to go to the bank and I'll go with you . . ." Eben's voice trailed off as Daniel lifted his eyes to his face.

"I can't take this," Daniel said, his voice rough.

"You can. You have to," Eben said flatly, leaning back in the chair and hooking an ankle over his knee. "You've lost that much money, easy, in the past year since I switched the health plans."

Daniel's eyes narrowed. "I haven't spent fifty grand over the past year," he said sharply.

"No? How come you sold your old house? Your Benz? And you're still in debt. Take the money. Pay off the doctor bills. Use it," Eben urged. "I know about Livvy's medicines, her health condition. I know she has to have surgery. Use the money."

The look in Daniel's eyes would live with Eben for the rest of his life . . . like some massive, painful weight had been lifted from him, setting him free.

She is the prettiest, funniest little girl, Eben thought later, as he let them talk him into staying for lunch. With those dark, large eyes dominating her face, and a sharp sense of humor that was already a match for her father's dry wit.

As Livvy ate slowly, she talked with Eben, about school, about Christmas. About herself.

"I'm sick," she said bluntly as her mother urged her to drink a little more, eat a little more. "Did you know that?"

Under her intent gaze, Eben shifted, feeling like he was being called in front of the principal or something. How could a child have eyes that wise? That mature? Softly, he said, "Yes. I know that."

"I have to have a surgery soon, or I'll die," she said baldly, wrinkling her nose up as she pushed the peas around on her plate.

Eben's eyes flew to her mother's face as the woman made a soft sound. "Mama," Livvy said softly, reaching out and wrapping her small fingers around her mother's hand. "I know about it. And I'm not too scared. But I'm going to be okay. I'll get the surgery and things will be fine. But I can't pretend like I don't know."

"It's always good to be prepared for things," Eben said, his voice tight and rusty. "But I bet it hurts your mama a lot to think about it."

Livvy glanced at her mama and sighed. "I know. I just . . . I don't like it when people act like I'm normal and healthy. So I want everybody to know."

Eben's heart went out to her, at the desolate look on her face, the wistfulness in her voice as she said, "I want to be normal . . . and healthy. I want to go back to my old school and I want to see my friends. But I can't. I have to be homeschooled, because I kept catching everybody's colds and stuff. And I can't go to the mall, can't go see movies . . . and all my medicines and my doctor visits cost so much money. Mama and Daddy think I don't hear them talking about it, but I know."

"Livvy," her father said gently, arching a brow at her.

"Well, I'm not going to act like I don't know why we sold the old house," the girl said, acting a little more like a child as she poked her lip out and sat back in the chair with her arms folded. "We just couldn't afford it there anymore. I know that's why you sold your car, and why you drive that old clunker."

Before Daniel could say anything, Eben leaned forward, propping his elbows on the table and staring at her. "Your mama and daddy don't care about those things, Livvy.

They care about you. And what's going on isn't your fault—sometimes there isn't anybody to put the blame on. You were born sick. Nobody made that happen, any more than they made you have the prettiest gray eyes I've ever seen, or gave your sister those pretty curls. That's just how it is. But that doesn't mean you're stuck with being sick . . . or stuck here."

By the end of the afternoon, Eben was convinced he was in love with the two little girls. When he went to leave, his eyes stung as both of them demanded a hug. A hug . . . had he ever hugged a child before?

Livvy felt so frail as he wrapped one arm around her shoulders, and the baby smelled so sweet, so innocent. Looking into her dimpled face, he felt something inside shift.

Clearing his throat, he handed Katie back to her mama before he walked outside into the cold, biting air. After Daniel promised to be at the office on Monday, Eben climbed into his car.

There was someplace else he needed to go . . . but he had to do something first.

Cara.

He had to go get Cara.

He was going to his cousin's house, finally, for the first time since his father had died. He was going to a family Christmas—and he wanted Cara there with him.

Cara wandered through the house, feeling bluer than she usually did on Christmas. For a while, there had been happy,

family Christmases for her . . . but since her parents died, she
had been going it alone.

She was so damned tired of being alone.

For a moment, she pouted. She would really have liked to
spend some more time with Eben today. Cara could have gone
with him—but if he had wanted her with him today, he would
have come.

And that thought just made her even more depressed. At
first it seemed like something was happening there . . .
her heart insisted something was happening. But if a guy
had feelings about you, wouldn't he want to be with you on
Christmas?

Yeah, she knew Eben didn't have a normal view of holidays
. . . but still . . .

As a knock sounded at the door, her breath caught and her
heart started to slam and dance inside her chest.

Maybe.

As Eben pulled into the small apartment complex where she
lived, he wondered at how his heart started to slam at the
thought of seeing her, how his gut tightened, his head spun . . .
how his cock hardened. She'd done this to him almost from
the get-go, and he had buried it, tried to ignore it, or shoved it
away, whatever seemed to work the best. He had even tried to
fuck her out of his system, that one night.

Fat chance. He could touch that sweet body for a thousand
years and he'd still want more. Crave more. But after just
one night, he'd tried to walk away. Tried to ignore that

nagging, insistent voice in his heart every time he had looked at her.

No more. He wasn't ignoring how he felt anymore. He wasn't going to focus on what his head was always whispering . . . he'd start listening to the rest of him.

Hell, if he had listened to his heart three years ago, he never would have pushed her away.

But three years ago, he wasn't sure he would have had a chance at keeping her. What happened yesterday, during the night, the visits from the ghosts had changed him. And maybe, just maybe, those changes would be enough to make her want to stay with him.

When she opened the door a few minutes later, the delight in her eyes struck him like a fist in the chest, knocking the breath from him. Forcing a smile, he said huskily, "I thought maybe you'd join me for dinner at a friend's."

As she reached out and threw her arms around his neck, Eben sighed, burying his face against her neck and just breathing in the scent of her. Her lips brushed his cheek and, blindly, he turned his face to hers, catching her mouth with his and tangling his tongue with hers.

In full view of everybody, he reached down and gripped her hips, boosting her up until she locked her legs around his waist for balance. Never taking his mouth from hers, he stumbled into the apartment and shoved the door closed with his foot as he turned and braced her back against the wall, pulling his mouth from hers and trailing a hot line of kisses down her neck.

Her hands raced up his shoulders to dip into his hair, holding the short strands eagerly as she pressed against his head.

He heard her whimper, low and soft, as he cruised down to kiss her nipples through the thin cotton of her nightshirt. Reaching for the hem, he caught it and pulled it over her head, grinning wolfishly as he found her all but naked underneath.

"Maybe I can have a snack first," he whispered, dipping his head to catch one stiff, deep rose nipple in his mouth, drawing the tight flesh inside, and sucking roughly.

Her fingers were busy on his jeans and she giggled, a light, happy sound, as she freed him from his shorts, his cock springing out, hard, thick, a tiny bead of moisture seeping from the tip as she cupped her hand around him.

"You know, we should be tired by now. We should have had enough, after last night," she said, grinning down into his eyes as he dropped to his knees in front of her.

He pulled away, letting her nipple leave his mouth with a wet little pop as he sat back on his heels, staring at the pale length of her body, wearing nothing more than a pair of forest green lace panties.

And Tinkerbell slippers.

He grinned at the slippers before he pulled off first one, then the other. Tossing them over his shoulder, he looked at her and smiled. "I won't ever get tired of you, of this . . . I won't ever have enough," he told her, leaning forward and pressing a closed-mouth kiss to her belly. "I could touch you for nineteen hours out of every damned day and still not have enough."

"Nineteen?" she teased. "Why nineteen?"

He grinned wolfishly. "Well, I do have to let you sleep a little."

His hands cupped her ass and he guided her down, staring

into her face as she slowly lowered her weight onto him, taking him inside and locking her ankles just above the hard curve of his ass. Eben shifted a little, stretching his legs out in front of him, bracing his shoulders against the wall before cupping his hands around her waist.

He tugged and she slid down, straddling his hips, rising up until only the merest fraction of his length was inside her, and then she pushed down, taking him back inside with one quick, hungry thrust as she covered his mouth with hers.

Eben cupped her ass in his hands and started to pump her up and down, groaning as she wiggled against him, arching her back so that her tight nipples stabbed into his chest. She laughed and grinned at him wickedly just before she started to subtly flex the muscles in her pussy, caressing his cock with slow, maddening contractions. "You're mean," he whispered, dipping his head to catch one rosy pink nipple in his mouth. "Teasing me like that."

She laughed at him, and the look of pure joy in her eyes struck him in the gut like a cannonball. "Think of it as your punishment," she teased, swiveling her hips against his as she continued that internal massage of his dick. Cream flowed from her as she rocked him, and Eben clenched his teeth, swearing as the fiery heat slid down to coat his balls.

"It's hard, but I'll take it like a man," he panted out, lifting her svelte form in his hands, then dragging her back down, shuddering as a spasm tore through her sheath, making her pussy tighten around his cock like a fist.

"Good boy," she teased.

He laughed harshly. "You should have waited before you said that. I'm not going to be good, after all," he told her, just before he rolled, flipping her onto her back and catching her behind the knees, draping her legs over his shoulders. Then he proceeded to fuck her, hard and slow, staring down at her face as her eyes flew wide and her mouth opened in a small O. He stroked deep inside the tight channel of her pussy, grimacing as she convulsed around him. Her hands fell limply to her sides, her head falling back, lashes closed as her body started to tense and shake under his. "Eben . . . please . . . oh, damn it, please . . . harder, just like that . . . oh, oh!" she screamed just before she flew apart underneath him, her pussy gripping his cock like a silken vise, tears sliding out from under her lashes.

Eben growled out her name, slowing his thrusts until he was barely rocking inside her, waiting for her eyes to open again. "I love watching you come," he whispered as she opened her heavy-lidded eyes to stare at him. Then he started to pump inside her, still hard, still aching. "I want to watch it again, and again . . . and again."

Sweat poured from their bodies as they lay on the floor of the small hallway, cold air seeping in from under the door to stroke teasingly along their shifting bodies. Eben arched his back, driving his cock deep and hard inside her, shuddering as she screamed out his name, reaching up and raking her nails across his chest. Hot fiery trails of sensation lingered where she had scratched him, and he burned everywhere they touched, so that his entire body felt like an inferno, just waiting to erupt.

As she once more started to buck and sob under him, his cock buried inside her swollen pussy, the silken, soft tissues convulsing around the steel-hard length of his sex, he came, pumping his come into the fiery depths of her pussy, her name falling from his lips in a hoarse shout.

Later, as she snuggled against him on the floor, he reminded himself they had a dinner to get to. Well, if they were late, it wouldn't matter too much. Joshua would welcome him with open arms, and in time, his wife would hopefully forgive Eben for being a bastard.

But right now, he had all he wanted in the world . . . It was Christmas night, and he had Cara.

Unwrapped

Lacey Alexander

This story is dedicated to my readers.
Your support means the world to me!

December 1

Simon's skilled hand eased beneath the sheet—and then between Emily's thighs. She parted them, whispering, "I love you."

"I love you, too, sugarplum," he said, his voice both sexy and teasing. He'd called her that ever since they'd met, three years ago, at a mutual friend's Christmas party. When they'd said goodbye that first night, he'd told her visions of sugarplums would be dancing in his head, and the pet name had been born. Then again, she'd always thought his Australian accent made *everything* he said sound sexy.

"Move against my fingers," he instructed her, the words coming low and throaty.

His touch felt *so* good, radiating through her in ribbons of heat, but she *wasn't* moving against his hand, at least not automatically, like she supposed most women would. She never had.

She could scarcely understand it. She *adored* being close to Simon, yet . . . sex always embarrassed her to a large degree. She'd never been able to completely let herself go.

Now, she tried to lift her pelvis against his touch.

His fingers stroked deeper and the sensation spread outward, through her rear, her legs, the small of her back. Oh God, it felt so wonderful, beginning to take her over, own her. *Yes, oh yes. Touch me, Simon.*

"That's right, my sugarplum girl. Fuck my fingers."

Emily sucked in her breath as her muscles tightened instinctively.

Oh damn. Why? Why, when he talked like that, did it at once arouse her and yet stop her dead in her tracks? In most other ways, she saw herself as a smart, confident woman, yet sex consistently filled her with conflicting emotions she didn't know how to fight.

She went still—and Simon sighed. "Sorry," he said, but his tone echoed his frustration. Which, in turn, made her feel guilty and inadequate. A familiar pattern.

She answered his sigh with one of her own. "I'm sorry, too, Simon. I don't mean to be this way—you know I don't."

He peered at her through the darkness—she always made a point of turning out the lights for sex—his handsome face somber in the shadows. "It's not your fault if I don't excite you." Then he rolled to his back in the bed and, despite her qualms, she missed having his hand between her legs.

Her chest had hollowed at his words, so she turned on her

side to press her palm to his bare shoulder, instantly needing to assure him. "Simon, it's not you—it's me."

A fact they both knew very well. She'd been a virgin at the ripe old age of twenty-three when they'd met. And he'd been so tender and gentle, slowly coaxing her desires free. When they'd finally made love nearly a year after meeting, it had been the sweetest, most profound experience of Emily's life. And she'd been so thankful to find a man so patient, so caring—caring enough to wait, and caring enough to put up with her inexperience and nervousness.

In short, Simon was amazing.

And she was a letdown.

Now, two years after giving him her virginity, and a year after moving in together, she just wasn't getting any better at sex. And it wasn't that she didn't want it—her body *burned* for him. It was simply that she'd been raised by very old-fashioned parents who had taught her she had to be a good girl . . . or else.

She wasn't sure what came after the "or else," what would happen if she *wasn't* a good girl—she'd never deigned to find out. But it was ingrained in her soul-deep, always had been. And even if her body *begged* her to move against Simon's hand, even if something deep inside her sparked to dirty life when he said the word "fuck," there remained a large part of her that simply couldn't seem to let go of being a good girl at the core.

And now she was afraid she would lose him.

Out of bed, they got along fabulously and were everyone's favorite couple. They shared a passion for hiking and long drives in the country and quaint little bed-and-breakfast hideaways, and they'd taken a fabulous road trip across the country—all the way from their home in Cincinnati to San Francisco—last summer. He supported the work she did as an advocate for the homeless, even though she didn't make much money, and she was proud of the way he was swiftly moving up the ranks of his prestigious downtown accounting firm. She'd even learned to enjoy soccer and basketball, his favorite sports. She remained thrilled to be the woman on his arm for any event, be it a fancy company banquet with his coworkers at Crain and Wilborn or a charity auction she had organized through *her* work.

But sex mattered. She knew that. Sex was important to men, plain and simple.

And really, it was important to her, too—she just . . . hadn't quite been able to express that. It was as if a vixen lay trapped in the body of a nun, struggling—unsuccessfully—to get out.

She kissed his chest, once, twice. Soaked up the warmth of his skin. As his arms closed back around her, she relished his strength and felt her body surge with the moisture of wanting him. "I'll try harder," she whispered, and she meant it.

Normally, Simon would argue now, tell her that she didn't *have* to try harder, that he loved her just as she was, that their sex was fine.

Yet this time he stayed quiet—and it didn't even hurt, because she knew he was entitled to more than she gave.

Maybe he even senses it—the way I want to be, the vixen lurking inside me. Oh God, I wish I could be the lover he deserves.

Now, she supposed, was her chance to try.

As she kissed her way down his chest, onto his stomach, a fresh yearning grew. Especially when her arm brushed over his erection under the covers. *Oh.* He was so hard for her, so big. He felt so good when he was inside her, and she wanted him there now. *Tell him that. Just say it. He'd love it, and it would be a good start.*

Yet she couldn't—the words felt locked inside her.

Above her, though, Simon's breath grew soft, ragged. Because she was moving lower. And lower.

She'd kissed him there before, at his urging. On his cock. She could *think* of it that way, but she just couldn't *say* it, damn it. *Why, why, why?*

Don't worry about that now. Just go down on him. That's how he would phrase it—he'd ask her to go down on him.

Kissing lower, she finally reached it—his cock. She said it again in her mind, trying as hard as she could to desensitize herself to the word. *Cock, cock, cock.* She studied it in the shadowy darkness, trying to meld both her gut responses, even though they seemed at odds with one another—that his erection was at once beautiful . . . and utterly sinful. His shaft jutted so big, so prominent, so very close to her face.

But it's not sinful, she argued with herself. *He's a man, and that's what men have, and there wouldn't be babies if they didn't.* And it *was* definitely beautiful. She grazed her palm down its length, her chest tightening with pleasure when he moaned. She *loved* to make Simon moan.

"Feels so good, baby," he breathed, further exciting her.

I can do this, I can use my mouth on him.

She lowered one soft kiss to his arcing length. So hard against her soft lips, like kissing warm steel. The heat from it pooled low in her belly, spreading down between her legs. *Mmm, yes. I can do this.*

She kissed him again and again—soft, sweet and impassioned—edging upward on his shaft toward the head. She ran her fingers gingerly over the tip, wiping away the thick dot of moisture there—and listened to Simon's throaty plea waft over her. "Suck me, baby. Suck my cock."

Inside her, just like before, everything tightened. Simon was rubbing her bottom now as she bent over him from the side, the sensation radiating inward, but her age-old enemies were setting in. Nervousness. Awkwardness. Fear.

She let out a sigh. She wanted to take him in her mouth— but she couldn't, just couldn't, for reasons that ran too deep for her to understand.

Oh God. Why am I like this? Why can't I be a good lover?

She found herself backing away then, her whole body stiffening, until she lay beside him, wishing she were anywhere else besides in bed with a man whose desires she couldn't fulfill.

"I'm so sorry, Simon," she whispered. "Forgive me."

"Of course," he said, voice quiet, strained.

He's lying. He doesn't forgive me.

"I want you," she said.

"It doesn't feel that way."

"I do. I swear." It was true. Unbelievable to him, probably, but so true.

"Please," she said, rolling to touch his chest again. "Please— I want you inside me. I love you so much."

Simon looked at her in the shadows, but she couldn't read

his expression. A certain darkness lingered there. Heated desire? Or disgust with her flip-flopping routine?

Either way, he rolled over onto her, situating himself between her parted legs. He kissed her neck, and as always when he did that, passion fluttered inside her once more. She did want him, she truly did. And as he pushed his way into her body, filling her, she groaned with the wonderful intrusion, reaching to meet his lush mouth with her own.

Things were different—so much more effortless—when he was on top of her, when he asked nothing of her, expected nothing. Maybe it just meant she was a selfish lover, she didn't know. But now that he was inside, she felt his renewed heat and saw it burning in his eyes. Now that he was inside, he was hot for her again, and *she* was hot for *him*, and the world was suddenly perfect.

"I love you, baby," she whispered.

"I love you, too. I want to make you come."

Could any man be better than Simon? All this, and still he cared about her pleasure. More than she did, possibly, because . . . well, she didn't always climax, not even when he touched her there. His touch was scintillating, but she knew she thought too much, let her nervousness get in the way.

As was their routine—the only one she'd ever really allowed them to fall into—Simon eased back, still inside her but upright, onto his knees. Using his thumb, he found her clitoris and began to stroke. "Want to make you feel so good, my sugarplum girl," he murmured over her deeply, sweetly. "So, so good."

His soothing voice combined with the darkness to help her slip away to somewhere else completely. In her fantasy, Simon

held her down, gave her no choice, *made* her feel the pleasure. They were in a different time, a different world, where it
was okay for her to feel dirty, to feel the slick way his thumbs
stroked through her wetness even as his cock slid just as slick
into her opening, to relish the hot pressure that rose in her, the
fullness, the pleasure, the—*oh God!* "Unh!"

Despite herself, she cried out as the orgasm broke over her
quickly, heard her own high sobs as the pulses pounded through
her body, until finally she was dropped back in the bed, back to
here, back to now—torn between that weird sense of guilt and
the joy of having let go, even if just for a moment.

"So sweet, baby," he purred over her, then kissed her, once,
twice, his tongue mingling with hers—but then, short seconds
later, he began pounding into her, hard, harder.

Yes, oh yes! She loved his power, loved the way his thrusts
echoed through her whole being. Now that her climax had
passed and she'd come back to herself, she could no longer yell
her pleasure aloud, but inside, her screams were deafening.

"Watching you come," Simon said on a heavy breath, still
driving his cock deep, "gets me so hot . . . I can't hold back."

As he exploded inside her, she absorbed the hard plunges,
filled with warmth to know she'd taken him there—although
to her way of thinking, it was amazing she even aroused him at
all, given her behavior. So she hugged him tight, thankful she'd
made it through one more night of these weird, contradictory
desires and could now simply hold her man while he recovered in her arms.

Please don't give up on me, Simon. I love you so much.

December 6

Simon looked up over his plate of hors d'oeuvres, his cock responding at the mere sight of Emily walking into his office Christmas party. Her dress was simple, black with thin straps at the shoulders, but it showed plenty of gorgeous cleavage and hugged her sumptuous curves. Her dark hair was piled on top of her head in a glamorous yet messy style he thought worthy of a red carpet, baring her beautiful neck.

Most men, he supposed, wouldn't get a hard-on just from watching their girlfriends walk into a room. Most men, though, didn't have the conundrum that was Emily in their lives. Funny, smart, sexy and more than a little easy on the eyes, his Emily. But get her in bed and she was like a deer in head-lights.

He had no idea why, other than what she'd explained to him about being raised to be prim and proper. He couldn't seem to get it through her head that when you loved somebody, all that shit went out the window. Or it should, anyway. He swallowed back the little dart of disappointment that pierced his heart at the thought. They were perfect together—if he didn't count how much she seemed to dislike having sex with him.

Elegant jazz versions of favorite Christmas classics provided the background to the party. The lavish, oversize lobby of Crain and Wilborn had been draped in sparkling red and gold, the large tree in the corner done in the same color scheme and sporting elegant glass ornaments. People sipped wine and mixed drinks and held paper plates festooned with holly leaves. As Christmas parties went, it was pretty boring. Which might explain why every eye in the place turned toward his sugarplum as she crossed the floor toward him. She had no idea what a knockout she was.

"Sorry I'm late." She smiled up at him, then helped herself to a shrimp puff from his plate.

He leaned down to kiss her. "You look incredible. Glad you're here."

She gave him a once-over that stiffened his cock a little more. "You look pretty incredible yourself."

He shrugged, but appreciated the compliment. "Just my everyday work attire, sugarplum." A crisp black Armani suit with a red tie, chosen that morning with the holiday in mind.

"But you wear it so well," she said.

And damn, if he didn't know better, the look in her pale blue eyes would make him think she was feeling hot, seductive.

His gaze dropped to her breasts, their rounded inner curves

revealed by the clingy dress. He wanted to slide his cock into that perfect valley. He was tempted to tell her that. With most women, after three years together, he'd be able to say that if he wanted, whisper it in her ear, a promise for later. But with Emily, he bit his tongue. She'd probably faint if he told her what he wanted to do with her breasts right now. At the very least, she'd turn fifty shades of red.

Just then, his colleague, Mark Wagner, sauntered up. Tall and lean like Simon, but olive-skinned with darker hair, Mark was a handsome flirt, and half drunk from the looks of him. "Long time, no see, Em," he said, then planted a palm firmly at her hip, leaning in for a slightly-too-long kiss on the cheek.

Damn. Even watching some other guy put the moves on his girl added to the stiffness in Simon's pants.

"Hi, Mark—how are you? Is Carolyn coming? Or are the twins keeping her too busy?"

Simon smiled. *Nice move, sugarplum.* She'd asked the questions in a completely sweet, confident tone, but they'd struck home, reminding Mark she knew exactly how much of a family man he was and that he should probably be keeping his hands and lips to himself.

Mark straightened, looking slightly cowed. "Yeah, Carolyn should be here any time now—had to drop the girls at her mom's first."

"Good—I look forward to seeing her," Emily said.

Simon forgave himself for having dirty thoughts about his coworker's hands on her since, hell, their sex life was so bland and dry and awkward that he figured pretty much *anything* would arouse him at this point. He knew Emily was as troubled by their different tastes in sex as he was, but it was wearing on him lately.

Just then, his boss and friend, Cal Hanson, walked up and slapped him on the back. "Drink up, buddy—life doesn't offer an open bar just every day."

Simon laughed. Cal, unlike him, possessed a sex life to be envied—and he liked to tell Simon about it, forcing him to suffer through tale after tale of seduction and debauchery.

Single and thirty, the same age as Simon, Cal had a knack for finding girls with sexual appetites and whims toward the kinky that Simon could only dream of. One of Cal's many girlfriends had recently dressed up in a French maid costume and cleaned his condo in between fucking his brains out. And it hadn't even been Halloween.

Nope, on Halloween Cal had gone to a wild party dressed as a sheik and come home with not one, but two hot harem girls who had taken turns pleasuring him, and each other, all night long.

Simon didn't care about conquests or anyone cleaning for him—but he'd love to have a girl who was that wild and free. Was it possible to have a great relationship like what he shared with Emily and also have a wild, crazy, no-holds-barred sex life? Was he asking too much? Hell, he'd settle for *less* than wild and crazy—he'd be thrilled out of his mind if Emily just gave him a blowjob, or let him eat her pussy. He'd gone down on her a couple of times, but she'd gotten all stiff and quiet on him and he'd known that instead of turning her on the exact opposite was happening.

Now he looked at the woman next to him who was expertly

chatting up his boss, clearly the envy of every other female in the office lobby. How could she be so very vibrant and exuberant—yet so distant and unhappy when they got naked together? It made no sense.

And the truth was, he wanted to take their relationship further—he and Emily had a great time together, they understood and respected each other, and in most ways, she embodied everything he could want in a woman. But sex—or the lack of it—was an issue for him. Maybe that made him shallow, but he couldn't deny that it put a damper on what they shared. Could he really be happy tying himself for life to someone who didn't enjoy sex?

He shook his head, banishing the thought for now.

Cal had just dragged Emily to the nearby bar, insisting she needed a drink—Simon heard him bellowing about the open bar again. So Simon took Cal's advice and drained his scotch and Coke, ready to get another himself—when Dana Landers grabbed his arm.

He looked into her dark eyes, but his gaze automatically dropped farther, to the deep V of the red cocktail dress she wore. Her large breasts were very much on display, and whether he liked it or not, it added to his erection. He hoped like hell his reaction didn't show on his face. "Hi, Dana—having a good time?"

She tilted her head, her expression playful and seductive. Dana had been flirting with him since she'd started working at Crain and Wilborn six months ago. Now, she rubbed his arm through his suit. "Kind of. But to tell you the truth, I'm in the mood for another kind of party altogether."

He slanted her a wary grin. "What kind of party is that?"

She let out an enticing sigh, her breasts heaving with the gesture. "The private kind. Cerise and I"—she motioned to another girl from the office, a recent college grad and blond beauty who he knew was also a cheerleader for the Bengals— "were thinking of heading back to my place and we were hoping you might want to come with."

Simon peered down into her eyes and took in the scope of the invitation. As starved as he felt for hot, no-inhibitions sex . . . Well, he'd never done the threesome thing himself, but if he didn't have Emily, he knew he'd be doing it tonight. Both girls were majorly hot and his cock now officially throbbed with the dirty visions entering his mind of him with two sexy babes who knew how to have fun in bed.

But he *did* have Emily, and even if she hadn't stood just a stone's throw away, he wasn't a cheater. He spoke kindly, though. "Dana, you know I have a girlfriend." He punctuated the comment with a lift of his eyebrows and a scolding grin.

She smiled boldly, unashamed. "We don't mind."

"But I do, I'm afraid. And besides, she's here tonight." He found himself pointing Emily out, still at the bar. "Black dress, talking to Cal."

Dana studied her. "Wow, she's hot." Then she lowered her chin provocatively. "She could come along, you know. Cerise and I aren't greedy."

At this, Simon just laughed. Both at Dana's flexibility and how much Emily would freak out if he even told her about the suggestion.

But then a picture entered his head. Him and Emily sitting on a sofa at Dana's place, watching Dana and Cerise fool around. Would that excite her? In the little fantasy in his head, it would turn Emily crazed with need. She would be so aroused that she'd lift her dress, straddle him, and fuck him, right in front of the other girls. She'd pant and moan and ride him hard, and she'd be so fucking beautiful doing it that he'd probably drop to his knees and beg her to marry him right on the spot.

Sweat broke out on his brow, but not exactly from excitement. Shit, how had his hot fantasy led to ideas about a *marriage proposal*?

He sighed. Probably because it had been on his mind lately. He really wanted to spend his life with Emily—if only she liked fucking him more.

He blew out a heavy breath as he refocused on Dana and her inviting cleavage. "Tempting, honey, but afraid we'll have to pass." Then he bent closer. "Here's a tip, though. Try Cal. He's into that kind of partying."

Dana looked disappointed. "It's really *you* I wanted."

He—and his dick—couldn't help being flattered, but . . . "Sorry, Dana—afraid that's just not our scene."

No, our scene is to do it in the dark, in the missionary position, once every couple of weeks or so.

He couldn't help thinking Dana would be *really* disappointed if she knew *that*.

"Well then," she said, "I guess I'll go see if you're right about Cal."

Ah, way to be a trouper, honey. "Don't worry, I am."

An hour later, Cal and the two girls had departed, and Emily and Simon had chatted with most of his coworkers. Music still played and alcohol still flowed. Emily always charmed anyone she came into contact with and this gathering was no exception.

Unfortunately for Simon, though, just watching his sugarplum charm people was enough to keep him aroused. Good thing he had his suit jacket on and buttoned, or everyone would know he wanted to take her, right in the middle of the red and gold lobby and expensive snacks. He wanted to start by kissing that long, slender neck. Then he wanted to lean into her from behind, let her feel his cock pressing into her ass as he reached around to cup her soft breasts. He wanted to push up that sexy little dress and drive his erection deep into her sweet, hot cunt.

Which was almost always wet for him. That's what stumped him. She was always wet, always ready—even when she was shying away from anything beyond that damn missionary position. If she was so disinterested in sex, why was she always so nice and moist when he reached inside her panties?

He looked at her now as she spoke with Mark Wagner's wife, who apparently wanted to donate some money to help the homeless and had asked Emily for advice on the best route to take. Finishing another scotch and Coke, he asked Emily if she'd like another glass of wine. She looked up, drawn from her conversation. "Oh—yes, Simon, thanks."

So off to the bar he went, thinking to drown his sorrows. *If I were a worse sort of guy, I could be sandwiched between two naughty girls right now.* A jazz version of "Santa Claus is Coming to Town" played overhead, reminding him 'twas the season to be deemed naughty or nice. Just his luck to fall for the nice girl.

On the way back from the bar, he realized Emily was

nowhere in sight. "Where'd she go?" he asked Carolyn Wagner.

Mark's wife pointed. "That way—looking for the restroom. Only, after she'd gone, I realized it's—"

"In the other direction," Simon finished for her with an easy grin. "Don't worry, I'll track her down. Watch these for me?"

"Sure," she said as he lowered their drinks to the table where she sat.

Pushing through the door that led to the firm's offices, he spotted Emily walking toward him, looking pretty—and a bit tipsy from wine consumption. "There are no bathrooms back here," she said, motioning vaguely over her shoulder as a short giggle escaped her.

He couldn't help smiling. "No, sugarplum. But look what's right *here*."

He moved forward to meet her next to Dana's office doorway, where a sprig of greenery and white berries hung. Emily glanced up. "Is that mistletoe or something?"

He gave her a playfully scolding look. "Of course it's mistletoe. Do you mean to tell me you've never seen mistletoe before?"

"I guess not."

"Well, you at least know what it's for, I hope."

She nodded invitingly. One thing about Emily—she might not like sex, but she loved to kiss.

At that, Simon slid his arms around her waist and stepped up close to her.

"Is that a Christmas present in your pocket or are you just happy to see me?"

He laughed, but gazing down into her eyes turned him serious just as fast. "The latter."

"Mmm," she purred as he molded his mouth to hers, easing
his tongue inside. Her arms curved around his neck as their
bodies settled closer together, his erection pressing to the
juncture of her thighs.

One kiss turned into two, then more, as their tongues lazily
sparred. He kneaded her hips, then her sweet round ass full
in his palms, and wondered if she could feel his cock getting
harder and harder against her. He'd been so damn aroused
all evening, all week—hell, for the last three years—that he
wanted her madly, wanted to make his little office party fantasy come true here in the privacy of the hallway.

Would she let him? Or would she bring their passion to a
grinding halt as usual? Only one way to find out.

He let his kisses drop to the pale expanse of her neck,
pleased when she leaned her head to one side, offering him
easier access. "So pretty, my girl," he breathed in her ear. "Hot
and beautiful. You make me the envy of every man here."

She bit her lip, turning to gaze up into his eyes. "Really?"

He nodded. "You're a gorgeous woman, Em. And I'm a
lucky, lucky man."

And if there's any justice in the world, about to get luckier.
He eased one palm to gently cup her breast through the dress,
listening to her heated sigh. Slowly massaging the weight of it
in his hand, he stroked his thumb over her beautifully beaded
nipple.

She gasped—but it wasn't her "stop" gasp. No, this was more
of an "oh yeah" kind of gasp. So he passed his thumb over that
sweet, hard peak again, this time catching it between thumb and

forefinger as he deepened their kiss, easing his tongue more fully into her mouth. She responded, arching, thrusting her breast into his grasp.

There were a million things Simon wanted to do to her right now while she was so heated up, so willing. He wanted to lean her against the wall, push her dress to her waist, drop to his knees and lick her damp slit. He wanted to urge *her* knees to the carpet and slide his cock into her warm mouth. He wanted to take her into Mr. Crain's corner office at the end of the hall and fuck her on the CEO's desk with her ankles locked around his neck, her high heels clicking together each time he pounded into her.

But he had to take this slow. Any progress he ever made with Emily and sex was always a result of going slow.

"I love you," he reminded her, his voice coming raspy.

She whimpered through her pleasure that she loved him, too.

"And I want so much more of you, my baby."

No answer, but when he reached to pull the slinky strap of her dress off her shoulder, she didn't protest. The thin strap of her black bra came with it until he was reaching inside the cup to lift her breast free.

Another hot sigh echoed from his sugarplum's lush lips, but she didn't stop him, only watched as he lowered his mouth there, taking the erect pink peak in his mouth. Ah, damn, he loved being able to see her—her full, round breast, the deep mauve shade of her distended nipple, the passion on her face—loved the simple fact that they weren't in a dark room. He suckled her gently at first, then deeper, deeper, relishing the hardness on his tongue, wondering if she felt the sensation between her thighs. She moaned her pleasure and he used both tongue and lips on her, drawing, sucking, as if the taut pink bud were a little straw that stretched all the way to her cunt.

He kept waiting for her to say no, but she didn't. And his hands moved without thought or decision—massaging her ass, then gathering the silky black fabric in his fists until he could reach underneath. And then—oh God, yeah—he found her bare flesh in his hands and remembered how she wore thigh-high stockings with dresses because they were more comfortable, and thongs with clothes she feared might show a panty line. She was so fucking sexy and didn't even realize it.

Of course, the thong made it easy. Too tempting to resist. He eased his fingertips down the valley of her ass overtop the lace strip residing there, then eased two underneath and into her warm, drenching folds. She let out another hot gasp as he whispered deeply, "Wet like always for me, sugarplum. So fucking wet."

He pushed two fingers up into her, listening to her soft sob, feeling the way she moved, rubbing against his cock in front, fucking his fingers in back. Yeah, oh yeah—it was finally happening. She was letting herself feel good. She was letting him make it happen. He fucked her deeper with his fingers, harder, and the only sound was their breath, ragged and raspy in rhythm with their movements. And then, soon, came the *noise* of his fingers, of her drenching wetness as he thrust up into her sweet pussy. Ah God—that new sound was enough to make him tremble, nearly enough to push him over the edge. He had to get inside her—now.

That's when she grabbed his shoulders and spoke throatily.

"Simon, we should stop. Someone could walk back here any-time."

True enough—only one door stood between them and the party, and a big band rendition of "Jingle Bell Rock" echoed through, albeit muted. But Simon couldn't have cared less. He just wanted to fuck her. He wanted it more than he'd ever wanted anything in his life. He had to have her, had to sink his aching cock into her welcoming flesh. "I don't care," he told her. "This is too damn good."

"But . . ."

He eased her back through the doorway of Dana's office. "In here. This will be more private."

"But I can't," she said. And she still moved against him, on his fingers, but . . . those movements were decidedly slower now, more stilted.

Oh fuck. Fuck, fuck, fuck. She was going cold on him. Just when he'd been stupid enough to think . . . Just when he'd be-lieved she might really . . . *Shit.*

A few months ago, in this same position, he might have tried to cajole her, convince her, continue to excite and per-suade her. But something had just clicked inside him. He'd had enough.

And it wasn't just because she wouldn't fuck him here. He knew some women would go for that and some wouldn't, and not going for it wasn't a crime. It was *everything*—the whole fucking three years that he'd tried to be patient, tried to teach her, tried to make her want him, want more from their sex. It was that she'd just taken him so deep into arousal before pull-ing the plug on it that his cock physically hurt now.

He backed away from her, swearing under his breath.

"Simon, I'm sorry. But right here . . . it's too . . ."

He simply shook his head. He couldn't even talk to her right now, couldn't explain. His frustration ran too deep. "I'm leaving," he said.

"But—"

"I'll see you at home," he snapped, then turned and walked out through the door that led to the lobby.

He'd just left her standing there, and he didn't care. Maybe that made him a lousy guy, but he felt like he'd been teased, led on. One too many times. And he was damn tired of it.

If he had half a brain, he'd find out where Dana lived, get in his car and go *there*. Emily would never have to know. Or, hell, maybe he should do it and *then* tell her about it, when he was breaking up with her.

He loved Emily, but he loved sex, too, and he didn't know how much more rejection he was supposed to take.

Without another word to anyone milling about drinking their drinks and listening to their Christmas music, he strode through the lobby and out the glass doors toward the elevators, ready to quit being the good guy for a change.

Merry-fucking-Christmas to me.

December 12

Emily trudged along, shopping bags in hand, trying to wade through the crowd. She loved Christmas, had always loved all the traditions and festivities that came along with it, but massive gridlock in the mall she could live without.

As she turned a corner, a teenage boy moving at a jog completely sideswiped her without looking back.

"Excuse you!" she snapped over her shoulder.

Sheesh. She was more than a little grouchy.

And if she was honest with herself, she probably couldn't blame it solely on the holiday rush.

She was upset and worried about Simon. His office party had been almost a week ago, and they'd smoothed things over and made up, but the intensity of the argument still ate at her. She'd driven her own car to work the morning of the party, just as he had, and met him there after, so they'd have driven home separately anyway—but it was still hard to believe he'd just walked out on her, at *his* event. It wasn't like him.

He'd acknowledged as much when she'd gotten home, and they'd talked about his frustration, about her confusion over why she just couldn't enjoy anything but simple guy-on-top, girl-on-bottom sex—and sometimes even *that* was tense for her.

She wanted to believe the talk had helped—but they'd had the same discussion before. And Simon had seemed rather wooden ever since the party, coming home late and going to bed early most nights—basically, just avoiding her.

Trudging on through the mall, she remembered the first time she'd met Simon. Harry Connick, Jr. had been singing "I'll Be Home for Christmas" in the background, and Simon had been wearing a red and white Santa hat, clearly a little drunk and flirtatious as he handed out small gifts their party host had gotten for every guest. "You must be Emily," he'd said in that fabulous accent. "Which means this one"—he held out a small silver box—"is for you."

Their hands had brushed as she'd taken the gift and the sensation had fluttered down her thighs. "How did you know my name?"

"I was told Emily was the most stunning girl in the room. So that has to be you." Tall, lean, with brown professional-yet-stylishly-cut hair, Simon's confidence was evident and attractive. His crooked smile had given away his tipsiness, but his eyes had held the sexiest gleam she'd ever seen.

Maybe that was the problem. Simon was so sexual. You

could see that in him instinctively. It had drawn her, in an animal way, from the start. Only later, she'd remembered, realized, that even with him, she just wasn't an animal. She didn't know *how* to be. A couple of weeks ago, she'd thought of herself as a vixen inside a nun's body—now another analogy struck her and she thought of herself as a tigress inside a staid housecat. She knew how to purr and rub up against Simon, but she didn't know how to claw or growl or be wild.

And if all this wasn't dire enough, she had no idea what to get him for Christmas. Almost every other person on her shopping list was finished, but not Simon. And he was easy to shop for—he loved nice clothes, had flexible taste in music and enjoyed popular fiction. But this year, with all the stress and strife between them, she wanted to give him something special, different, unique. She wanted to find a gift that truly reflected the measure of her love for him—since she couldn't seem to show him in the normal way.

Oh God, I'm losing him. I'm really going to lose him. Because I have sexual hang-ups and can't get past them.

She let out a big whoosh of breath and realized she'd stopped walking to lean against a glass wall that fronted one of the stores. The deep realization that she was going to lose the man she was in love with had struck hard and made her feel as weak . . . as a kitten.

Just then, she felt a soft touch on her arm and glanced up.

"Dawn?" Before her stood an old friend from college who looked just as gorgeous as Emily remembered. Auburn hair still fell long and flowing over her shoulders, and a fitted top and jeans showed she still possessed a killer shape. Midnight-blue eyeliner made her green eyes look large and smoky. Dawn had always been very different from her—a wild child who, even back then, could have filled a book with her sexual exploits—but they'd been in the same dorm through all four years at the University of Cincinnati and had always gotten along well.

"Emily? I thought that was you. Are you okay?"

Caught off guard by the meeting, Emily straightened, tried to take control of herself. "Yeah—yes. I'm fine."

Dawn didn't appear convinced. "You looked like you might faint or something. Maybe it's too crowded for you in here."

Emily just nodded. "Could be." But then she sighed.

And Dawn's eyes narrowed. She'd always been especially perceptive. "Something else is wrong. What is it? Maybe I can help."

Emily gave her head a quick shake. She hadn't seen Dawn in years, and though they'd once been fairly good friends, she couldn't just spout out the trouble with her love life.

Except . . . the stress must have been worse than she even realized, because she heard herself doing it anyway. "I'm afraid my boyfriend is going to leave me."

Dawn's feminine hands closed on her upper arms. "Oh, *honey*," she said, her voice filled with compassion.

Emily rolled her eyes. "My God, I can't believe I just told you that. I haven't even said 'How are you?' yet."

But Dawn simply laughed, her heart-shaped lips widening into a smile. "Don't worry about it. And I'm fine—better than you are, apparently." She shifted from one platform heel to the other. "Listen, why don't we get out of here. Go to my place. I'd love to catch up. And you can tell me all about this guy of yours and what the problem is—and who knows, maybe talking about it will do some good."

Dawn lived in the trendy neighborhood of Mt. Adams, in a condo atop a three-story building that overlooked the city through a wall of windows. The place was decorated in lavish fabrics and jewel tones, a purple velvet chaise draped with a red chenille throw serving as one of the most outstanding pieces of furniture in the large living room. Dark wood trim and a fireplace added to the warm feel of the space, in which the only holiday decoration was a small, unobtrusive tree in one corner done in matching jewel tone ornaments. Emily couldn't help thinking it would be a great room to have sex with Simon in.

Which confused her, all things considered. Then again, she figured the thought blended with her usual state of sexual turmoil.

Over hot chocolate laced with brandy to warm them up after coming in from the cold, Emily found herself telling Dawn about Simon, and about her problems in bed. She didn't know why she found Dawn so easy to talk to, but her old friend had always had a way of gently coaxing honesty from her. Of course, maybe the brandy helped, too. Either way, she heard herself telling Dawn things that, for some reason, she hadn't quite been able to tell Simon.

"It's like . . . my body is just teeming with all this desire, but my brain tries to turn it off—and usually succeeds."

Dawn leaned forward on the leather sofa they shared to

touch Emily's knee. "Is it *fear* you feel when he urges you to try new things? Or some kind of *shame*?"

Emily swallowed, thinking it over—wanting desperately to figure it out, finally. Something about Dawn's soothing voice, the comfort of her touch, the cozy setting—plus the brandy's ability to relax her—made her feel close, so very close, to finally digging beneath the surface of her troubles and really reaching an answer. "Fear of the unknown is definitely a part of it. And yet, another, wilder part of me that I can't quite reach really *wants* to try these things, really wants to learn."

Dawn flashed a sympathetic expression. "So you've *really* never given a guy a blowjob? Or had sex in any position besides missionary?"

Emily didn't feel embarrassed by Dawn's surprise over the secrets she'd already shared—just sad. "No, never. I really *want* to—just thinking about it excites me inside. But when I try to actually do it, I just freeze up. I guess . . . I guess maybe it *is* some kind of shame—although I never thought of it like that before. It just feels . . . wrong somehow. Not inside my heart, but in my head."

Dawn lowered her chin and widened her eyes, looking inquisitive. "Just how strict *were* your parents, honey?"

Emily bit her lip, remembering. She didn't particularly like thinking about it. "They were *very* strict when it came to boys. I couldn't date until I was seventeen, and even then, they filled me with terror about letting a guy touch me at all, or kiss me. I remember being a nervous wreck. Even before that, though, if we were watching TV and anything at all sexual came on, my mother changed the channel. We just never talked about sex in our house, unless I was being warned not to do it. Even the *topic* embarrassed me at the time because it seemed so taboo."

"And you were an only child, right?"

Emily nodded. "So I didn't have anyone to talk to about this stuff. Girlfriends, sure, but no one really understood why the very idea of sex freaked me out so much, because they didn't see what it was like to live with my mom and dad."

"Was it . . . a religious thing for them?"

"Not really. We went to church, but . . . well, I think maybe my mom was sexually abused when she was younger. She's never said so—but once my aunt told me I had no idea what my mother had been through and that I just had to be patient about not being allowed to date. Since we didn't talk openly about anything like that, I never asked her. But whatever the reason, she and my dad both definitely wanted to shield me from anything sexual."

Next to her, Dawn swallowed a sip of her hot chocolate and sighed. "This is making more sense to me now. Some people who are abused handle it well and raise their kids in a sexually healthy way. But some don't."

Emily widened her eyes. Dawn sounded so . . . knowledgeable. "And you know this how?"

Dawn smiled. "I should have told you this already, but I didn't want to intimidate you. We kind of moved right past the normal chitchat today, so it didn't come up, but . . . I'm a sex therapist, Emily."

Emily held in her gasp. Although maybe she shouldn't have been surprised, given Dawn's affinity for sex when they were younger. "Wow. What does a sex therapist do, exactly?"

"What you would expect, mostly. I counsel couples and

individuals who are having sexual problems. We try to get to the root of the problem and then see if we can find solutions or at least ways to improve the situation." Then a coy smile formed on her pretty face. "And since I'm getting a little drunk on the brandy here, and since we're old friends, I'll tell you that I have, on occasion, served as a sexual surrogate, too."

Emily blinked, but tried not to look too shocked. "Meaning you . . ."

"Have sex with someone who needs the kind of help that only direct, personal instruction can provide."

"With men," Emily said, to clarify, although she had no idea why.

Dawn quirked a sexy grin in her direction. "Women, too, sometimes."

"Oh." Her voice fluttered.

Dawn touched her knee again. "Don't worry. I wasn't suggesting I'd do that with *you*." She spoke slower then. "Although I would. If you wanted me to."

Emily immediately shook her head and looked down, suddenly unable to make eye contact. "Oh, no. I would never, could never . . ." Her heart beat too fast.

Facing her on the sofa, Dawn lifted Emily's chin with her fingertips and looked deep into her eyes. "Listen to me. This is lesson number one. You have to quit being embarrassed about sex. You have to maintain eye contact. It's *just* sex. Just how people show their affection for one another. It's both natural and normal."

Emily swallowed, intensely aware of Dawn's soft touch beneath her chin, and worked to keep looking into her shadowy green eyes. After a few seconds, it got easier.

"See?" Dawn's voice remained *so* soothing. "It's not so hard to look at me, is it? It's not so hard to talk about."

Emily let out a trembling breath. She wished she hadn't just gotten so nervous—she *hated* that feeling. She reminded herself that this was just Dawn, her old friend.

Of course, now she knew Dawn had sex with women. But even so, she was still Dawn, and Emily was comfortable with her. "No. You're right."

Dawn smiled. "Good. Now take another drink. Let it relax you."

Emily complied, and the brandy warmed her chest as she emptied her mug.

"And now, keep looking at me, Em, and tell me you want to talk about sex."

"I want to talk about sex." Okay. That was easy.

"Tell me you want to learn how to please your man."

Easy again, because it was so true. "I want to learn how to please my man."

"Tell me you want to be totally at ease with him."

"I want to be totally at ease with him." She was getting good at this, maintaining eye contact, *feeling* the words as she said them.

"When he touches you," Dawn said, clearly intending Emily to keep repeating.

"When he touches me."

"When he fucks you."

Emily drew in her breath, shut her eyes. Then opened them. "Words like that . . . I can't seem to say."

Dawn's mouth made a straight line across her face, but she didn't look surprised. Maybe she'd encountered this

before. "They're only words, Emily. Sounds. Letters put together."

"They're . . . dirty to me."

"Dirty can be a very good thing."

Emily understood that on some level, understood in those
brief moments when she let herself feel naughty that she also
felt . . . alive, free, wild, wonderful, in a way she never had before. "Maybe so, but . . ."

"Say *fuck* for me."

When Emily didn't do it, Dawn persisted. "Say it. Just say it.
It's only a word. It can't hurt you."

Emily swallowed nervously. "Fuck," she whispered.

"Was there anything horrible about that?"

She sighed. "No. No, not really."

"No, of course not." Her friend spoke gently. "But there *can*
be something very good about it. Simon will love it when you
ask him to fuck you, I promise. Words can excite and please
a man *so* much. They show him you want the same things he
does, with the same force, the same deep need. Now, say it
again. But in a sentence. Say *fuck me*."

Emily drew in her breath. "Fuck me."

She was looking right at Dawn as she spoke, brutally aware
that it sounded as if she were making the demand to her
friend. But Dawn only smiled. "Very good. Now, *fuck me,
Simon*."

Emily's chest burned with trepidation and a strange heat.
Her throat felt heavy, thick. She said the words slowly, her
voice low, and felt them in her soul. "Fuck me, Simon."

Dawn nodded, and Emily's chest tightened. "Mmm, yes.
That's nice," Dawn said.

Oh God, was she crazy or did her friend actually appear kind of aroused? Emily's heart beat harder and her breasts tingled.

But then, thankfully, Dawn's intense gaze dropped to the empty mug Emily still held. "More?"

More brandy? Probably a good idea. "Yes. Thanks." Or at least she *thought* it was.

As Dawn moved to the open kitchen flanking the living room, an area filled with equally warm colors of dark yellow-gold and burgundy, she said, "I want you to practice after we've parted. Practice saying *fuck*. Practice saying *pussy*. Practice saying *cock*."

"I've been practicing *that* one a little already," she admitted. *At least in my head.*

Dawn giggled throatily. "Good." She went about heating the hot chocolate in the microwave, then adding quick splashes of brandy into the two steaming mugs. "Work on them in sentences, too. Become comfortable with them. Being comfortable with words gives you power, control."

She returned to the leather sofa, passing Emily's mug. Emily blew on the chocolate as the ceramic warmed her palms, and she told herself she could do this—she could learn to talk dirty for Simon.

She looked up, surprised to see Dawn lower her cup to a coaster, then promptly disappeared through a nearby doorway. "Be back in just a minute," she said over her shoulder. "Get ready for lesson two."

"Which is?" Emily called.

"Touching."

Emily gulped, her body seemed to deflate a little from

shock. "Um, touching?" Was Dawn going to . . . touch her? Or expect her to return the favor? Every fiber of her body recoiled instantly at the thought. Except . . . for maybe one or two.

Whoa. Oh *God*.

The *awareness* of those one or two more adventurous fibers, arriving with a tiny hint of curiosity that made the crux of her thighs pulse, shocked her more than anything in her life had up to now and made her breath hitch. Could she? Could she want that?

"I'm going to show you the joys of touching yourself," Dawn said, appearing in the doorway in a sexy bra and panties a moment later. Made of red lace with black ribbon trim, they hugged her snugly—thin black bows at both hips held the panties on. The tight bra barely concealed her nipples and revealed exactly how large and round and smooth Dawn's breasts were.

"Um . . ." Emily began, lost. The truth was, her whole *body* was tingling now—with excitement. She didn't like it, but she couldn't control it. At least Dawn wasn't suggesting they touch *each other*, but Emily's flesh still felt strangely supercharged, sensually energized in a way it never had before.

Dawn calmly smiled. "Here's where you work on relaxing again. Sip your drink. And don't look away from me. Get comfortable with things that are sexual." She moved in long, graceful strides to a plush red chair across from the couch where Emily sat sipping her hot chocolate madly. "Nothing turns a guy on more than watching a woman touch herself. It's the ultimate erotic act for them."

Emily drew the mug down from her lips. "Then, um, shouldn't we start with something a little tamer?"

A thick laugh escaped Dawn's throat and Emily wondered if her nipples were showing through her sweater. "No," Dawn answered. "Because once you've mastered *this*, the rest is easy. Get comfortable with touching yourself intimately and it will be easy to touch Simon that way, too. Learn to understand what your body needs and it will be easier to get it." She grinned. "Now, sit back, relax and watch. Don't be afraid, or embarrassed. Pretend you're just watching this on a screen, by yourself, in the privacy of your own home. Then, later, you're going to go home and do this yourself, okay?"

Fat chance. But Emily was numb. "Okay."

Sitting down in the soft red chair, Dawn spread her legs wide and ran her palms sensually up her inner thighs, then lifted one shapely leg to drape over the arm of the chair. Emily drank her hot chocolate, then bit her lip. The spot between *her* legs throbbed still more now, and when she felt the urge to look away, she took another drink instead and forced herself to keep watching.

Dawn smoothed splayed fingers up over her lace undies, then her silky, white stomach and onto her ample breasts. As she slowly kneaded, massaging them, she leaned back her head and sighed. Her eyes fell shut, her mouth went lax. And Emily's chest turned heavy, warm.

Opening her eyes again to peer over at Emily, Dawn reached behind her with both hands and, a second later, the bra loosened around her. Emily held her breath, for the first time in her life curious to see another woman's breasts.

The lace dropped away to reveal perfect round orbs, large and beautiful, that Emily thought might have been augmented. When Dawn met Emily's gaze, then took her bared breasts back in her hands, tweaking the dusky nipples between thumb and forefinger, Emily's *own* breasts seemed to swell within the confines of her sweater. At this point, she *couldn't* look away—she hadn't the power. She watched, transfixed. Aroused, curious, wondering if she could possibly ever touch *herself* that way, and if she could, could she do it in front of Simon? Did it feel good? Was Dawn's body humming right now, as Emily's was? Was it as arousing to touch yourself while someone watched as it was to be the one watching?

From there, Dawn dropped her hands to one hip. Sensually licking her upper lip, she slowly, teasingly pulled the black ribbon tied there. The panties loosened and Emily waited impatiently as her friend reached toward the other side. When the lace fell, revealing Dawn's vagina, Emily sucked in her breath. All the hair had been removed! It was so very on display! Pink flesh surrounded her soft, white skin.

"Do you ever touch your pussy, Emily?"

Oh damn, she was supposed to be thinking of it that way— as a pussy, not a vagina. "Um, no." Her gaze remained riveted on Dawn.

"You have to. Tonight. As soon as you leave here and go home. Promise me you will."

She let out a heavy sigh. "Um . . . okay." *But I don't really know how. Like Simon touches me?*

Only she need not have worried—she should have known Dawn was about to show her.

Her friend slowly dragged her middle finger, tipped with

a bright red nail, through the damp pink folds at her center. "Mmm," she purred.

Then she used *two* fingers, gently stroking, stroking, before concentrating her attention at the top of the open slit, on the clitoris. The clit, Dawn would surely call it, though. Emily tried to think of it that way, too.

Dawn rubbed two fingertips in rhythmic circles over her swollen clit and Emily found her own pussy burning more and more anxiously now and wished she could touch herself, too. She couldn't, of course—but at least she'd just thought of that part of herself as her pussy, so that was progress.

She watched raptly as Dawn continued to finger herself, her eyes falling shut again as she let out a low moan. Before long, she clenched her teeth, her self-caresses turning more fevered. Emily took a long chocolaty gulp of her drink, aware that the heady feeling of intoxication was making it much easier to watch, and to feel. Her pussy throbbed against the heavy seam of her blue jeans and she just barely resisted the urge to move around in her seat.

Dawn's breath came heavy, hot, the only sound in the room—and Emily's entire body felt imbued with still more of that new energy, an arousal unlike any she'd ever experienced.

"I'm gonna come," Dawn informed her, still breathing heatedly. "I'm gonna come hard."

And then she cried out—a short, loud sob followed by a series of low moans that made Emily's stomach contract with the intimacy she'd just unwittingly shared with Dawn. "Oh my God," she whispered, taken aback by it all. Such a private act, and yet she'd been there, witnessing it, getting excited by it.

Slowly, Dawn's body seemed to relax, until she finally

opened her eyes and refocused on Emily with a smile. "Was it good for *you*?"

"*Amazing*," Emily uttered.

"So you see how incredible it feels to watch. Just think of *Simon* feeling that way, watching *you*."

"Oh, I *want* that for him, because . . . wow, it *did* feel incredible. So hot and intoxicating and . . ." She trailed off, realizing she was gushing about how great it had been to watch Dawn climax. Dear God. She was *so* not a lesbian—what was happening to her? "Only, I mean . . ."

Dawn tilted her head, looking relaxed, happy, indulgent. "What *do* you mean?"

"Just that I'm . . . not into girls . . . that way." She was shaking her head.

As usual, though, Dawn simply laughed. "Doesn't matter. Sex is sex. You can't choose what arouses you. People work way too hard defining things like that, trying to analyze what every sexual reaction means—and fearing them. When they *should* just be enjoying themselves."

Emily sighed. "I wish I could be so . . . free about it all. Even *half* as free."

Naked, Dawn rose and walked to the sofa, kneeling on the carpet to place both hands on Emily's knee. "Tonight you'll go home, get yourself off, and realize how wonderful it is, and you'll be a big step closer to sexual freedom."

Emily looked down into Dawn's green eyes, and more honesty erupted. "I . . . I'm not sure I *can*. Make myself come, I mean."

"Weren't you paying attention? I hope you were watching

exactly what I was doing with my fingers—both for your sake and for Simon's."

"I was." *I definitely was.* "I just . . . don't always have orgasms very easily. Sometimes, sure—but other times, I just . . . can't quite get there." When Simon had made her come that night a couple of weeks ago, the speed and ferocity of it had been downright shocking—and that wasn't the norm.

Dawn drew back slightly. "The same old trouble? Feelings of it somehow being wrong?"

Emily tried to examine what she so commonly felt. "Something like that. Sometimes Simon touches me and I climax and it's great. But other times . . . I just can't feel what I'm supposed to. And the harder I try, the worse it gets. And I guess, yeah, it feels . . . shameful or something to . . . to become so . . . heated, to . . . lose myself that way, even for just a few minutes."

Dawn squeezed Emily's knee and the sensation shot to the crux of her thighs. "Poor baby," she said, looking truly sad for her. "You just have to change your mind-set. You have to know that there's nothing shameful in sex, or in getting off. You have to teach yourself that. You have to pretend you're learning about sex and orgasm for the very first time and then form new opinions, new feelings about it. Do you think you can do that?"

"I . . . can try." Given what she'd just let herself sit and watch, maybe she *could* do things she'd never thought she could before. She let out a sigh, though, still thinking of orgasms. What if she gathered the courage to touch herself in front of Simon, but then couldn't come? It would feel like the ultimate defeat to get that far and not be able to go all the way. "I'm still . . . worried about coming, though. Or . . . *not* coming, as the case may be."

Dawn pursed her lips thoughtfully. Then she reached up to take the warm mug still in Emily's grasp, lowering it to the coffee table next to her own. "Tell you what, honey. You go lie down on the chaise, okay?" Dawn pushed to her feet, taking Emily's hands in her own.

"Why?" Emily murmured, letting herself be drawn up from the sofa.

"I'm going to go throw something on and I'll be right back. Then we're going to work on relaxing you."

Emily nodded. Relaxing was good. And surely easier than watching Dawn masturbate.

So she pushed to her feet and meandered to the velvet lounge. Lying back, she took in the view of the city and the Ohio River beyond. A stark winter-white sky turned the whole scene slate-like, pale and cold, making her all the more relaxed by the warm atmosphere of the room.

When Dawn came back, she hadn't put *much* on—a short, slinky red kimono tied in front and stopping high on her thighs. She smiled. "Relaxed?"

"Trying to be."

Really, she thought she *was* beginning to calm down inside. Sure, she remained a little aroused by what she'd just observed so unexpectedly, and all this talk of sex and thoughts of being naughty with Simon—but the brandy was making it all too easy to sink fully into the luxurious chaise.

"Good." As Dawn stepped behind the plush lounge, her voice became even more soothing than usual. "Now close your eyes, Emily, and hear my voice. Concentrate on my words, nothing else." With that, she began to slowly, deeply massage Emily's neck and shoulders. The kneading sensation echoed through her like fingers of heat.

"Oh, that feels good," she moaned. Her muscles were stiff lately from too much time at the computer combined with toting heavy shopping bags and wrapping gifts.

"Like we discussed before, we need to teach you to relax and just feel, not think. Just let your body take in the sensations being delivered to it. Just let yourself do what feels good." Her voice dropped a bit lower then. "Watching me, for instance. Watching me touch myself felt good to you. Being able to see it, see my body, my expressions, my actions." Emily had admitted early in their conversation that she always turned the lights out for sex. "Visual stimulation is an important factor in arousal, Emily. The body is a beautiful thing, both the man's and the woman's. Again, there's nothing wrong with letting your body feel what it wants to feel. Especially if you have a sexy guy you love to do it with."

Emily voiced the thought that broke through her semi-relaxed state. "The problem is, I guess I'm afraid that . . . he has this idea of who I am now, and what if he doesn't like me as a wild, sexual woman?"

Dawn's chuckle flowed over Emily warm and confident. "Honey, I've yet to meet the man who doesn't like a wild, sexual woman." Then she paused before adding, "Do you remember, in *Grease*, when Sandy changed into a bad girl at the end? You still liked her, didn't you?"

"Actually, I thought she was abandoning her true self to please a guy."

Dawn laughed again, a more full-bodied sound this time. "Okay, fair enough. But the difference here is—you *want* to be sexual. It's *in* you. You've told me so. And just remember the look on Danny's face when he saw the new Sandy. He was thrilled—finally, she was everything he needed her to be. And if deep inside, you're *already* everything Simon needs you to be, you have to let that out. You can't waste another minute that you could be having hot fun with him, making him happy and growing closer all at the same time." Dawn's fingers still moved rhythmically over Emily's shoulders, her touch beginning to stretch down over her collarbone.

"You make this sound easy."

"Given where you're coming from, no, it's not easy at all. But it's worth it. If you don't open yourself up, you might never really be happy."

Emily let out a long, heavy sigh. Dawn's last words had just hit her square in the gut. Not just because she'd lose Simon if she didn't open up, but because she'd never really get to know her true desires, the things she really wanted. She'd never be the whole woman she could be. "You're right, Dawn—you're so right. I want to let go of all this silly baggage. I want to pleasure Simon. And I'm going to."

Just then, Dawn's kneading fingertips stretched farther, onto the tops of Emily's sensitized breasts. She felt the touch everywhere.

And her voice went softer. "I'm going to."

"That's so good, honey," Dawn said, her tone sweet, comforting. "Now . . . no more talking. Just feel. Just imagine my hands are *Simon's* hands. Just imagine you're alone with him, and afraid of nothing, letting your body do what it wants."

When Dawn's hands slipped down over both her breasts, Emily thought to protest, but she didn't. She was supposed to just feel. To teach herself it was okay. No more talking, Dawn had said. *Just feel. Just feel.* If she wanted to save her relationship with Simon . . . she had to just feel.

She clenched her teeth as pleasure spread through her chest and outward, downward. She tried to keep her breathing even, tried not to sigh with how good it felt. *This is Dawn, your friend, a* woman, *touching you sexually!* The thought rushed through her brain, but she held it at bay. *She's a sex therapist. She's helping you. Be quiet. Just feel.*

"Think of Simon," Dawn whispered, her voice barely audible. Emily's eyes remained shut, but she sensed Dawn moving around to the side of the chaise. Once there, she resumed gently kneading Emily's breasts, her soft touch drifting down to caress her stomach, too. "Think of pleasing your man. The hands on you right now are his. Think of his cock, Emily. Think of it big and hard, just for you. Think of taking it in your mouth, wanting it there, letting it fill you. Hear his moans when you slide your lips up and down, feel his fingers in your hair." At this, one hand left Emily's breast and threaded back through the hair at her temple, making her sigh.

"You want to please him so much, and you want to let him pleasure you, too. Think of him parting your legs with his hands." Dawn did that then, gently parted Emily's legs. "Think of him licking your pussy." She ran one finger smoothly up the center seam of Emily's jeans between her thighs. "Think of his mouth on you, giving you such raw pleasure." Dawn began to rub then, rub Emily's mound through the jeans. "Think of him licking and sucking your clit deep into his mouth . . . until you come for him, so hard."

When Emily felt the urge to lift against Dawn's touch, she didn't fight it. For once in her life, she didn't fight something that felt wild, crazy, a true act of hedonism. She wasn't into girls. She only knew it felt good. Like electricity zipping through her. She had to go with it, let it happen. Quit analyzing.

She followed Dawn's instructions—she thought of Simon. For the first time, the idea of his face between her legs didn't feel dirty or strange or wrong. She parted them wider, imagining his mouth on her, taking in as much of her pink flesh as he could. She thrust gently, her body swallowing the rhythmic pleasure—getting lost in it, not thinking, only feeling.

So good. So good. Oh, how she wanted Simon. She wanted to throw herself on him. Suck his cock. Then ride it. She wanted to touch her breasts for him—and so she let her hands glide upward, onto them, to gently squeeze. Her own nipples pushed through her bra and top into her palms. She thrust her pussy harder. She licked her upper lip. She held her breasts tighter. She didn't think, just felt, just moved, just reached—and then she came. It broke over her in startling waves of heat and light that devoured every other thought or sensation but all-encompassing pleasure. It moved through her like wildfire and nothing else existed. There was no shame, no guilt, no thought—only orgasm.

When finally it faded, she waited—for the guilt. Surely it would wash over her now, hard and heavy. After all—my God!—she'd just fooled around with a woman.

Only, the guilt didn't come. Dawn had somehow made all this seem perfectly normal, and simply therapeutic.

She opened her eyes and met Dawn's gaze. "I can't believe I did that."

Dawn only smiled. "I can. And my prognosis for you is that you're going to be just fine. So long as you let yourself."

When Emily left Dawn's condo a little while later, she felt a new kick in her step as she made her way to her car parked along the curb in front. Maybe after today she could do this. Maybe she could be what Simon *needed* her to be, what *she* needed her to be. She'd have to practice, have to teach herself, like Dawn said—she'd have to truly let go of the unhealthy sexual ideas her parents had ground into her and accept herself as the sexual being she was. But maybe she could do it. Hell, maybe she could even do it by Christmas if she worked really hard.

She glanced up at Dawn's front window with a smile, thinking, *Thank you*. And as she got in the car and pulled away, heading home, she had a feeling she knew what to get Simon for Christmas now.

Her, unwrapped.

December 18

Simon wandered out of a jewelry store into the madness of the mall, where he'd been shopping for a gift for Emily without success. Harried shoppers rushed to and fro all around him and Gene Autry sang "Rudolph the Red-Nosed Reindeer" overhead through hidden speakers. He usually *liked* Christmas. This year, though, not so much.

It was Emily. She'd seemed happy enough the last week or so, busy wrapping gifts and baking cookies and reminding him to wear the reindeer tie his mother had bought him last year—which he kept purposefully forgetting, since he liked the song okay, but just didn't think reindeer made a good fashion statement.

For her, it seemed as if that night at his office party had never happened. He only wished he could feel the same way. But he remained torn. He loved her, yet he just couldn't seem to move past their problems this time. And he knew it wasn't her fault—he knew this was all about the way her parents had raised her in a little farming community a few hours north of the city—but he also had grave doubts about whether they could truly be happy in the long-term when they felt so differently about something as big as sex.

Ahead, he spotted the big Santa display in the middle of the mall. Santa Claus sat in a large throne-like chair on a platform with mechanical reindeer scattered about and enormous round peppermint candies suspended on long cords from the ceiling far above. The little girl perched on Santa's lap cried while her mother made silly faces at her from behind the photographer.

Despite himself, the sight reminded Simon of the dream he'd had last night.

Like so many dreams, it was somewhat nonsensical—but he'd definitely liked it.

He'd been dressed up, playing a department store Santa himself. He'd never done that or had any urge to, but in the dream, it seemed normal. He sat atop a throne similar to the one before him now, but he'd been surrounded by a cottony, glittery winter wonderland scene—which he thought he should tell the mall personnel about, since he'd found it much more appealing than the plastic reindeer and oversize candy.

Other major differences between his dream and this reality: There had been no crowd in the dream, no one else around but the girl perched in his lap. And that girl hadn't been a child. She'd been Emily, wearing a red, see-through baby doll nightie and carrying a matching lollipop. She'd squirmed flirtatiously in his lap, sucking provocatively on the candy.

"Are you naughty or nice, little girl?" he'd asked in a deep Santa voice.

"Oh, definitely naughty," she'd assured him in a sexy tone he'd never had the pleasure of hearing Emily use.

And then the damn alarm had gone off, and he'd awakened to find one of Em's legs looped over his, which was both comforting and . . . frustrating. Given the dream. And the fact that he didn't have the luxury of rolling over and initiating some nice morning sex with her as he would have with most women.

She'd smiled at him, having no idea of his thoughts, or that his dick was hard. Happy as a clam these past days, his Em, and he had no idea why. The holiday spirit, maybe? He knew she was looking forward to the big dinner she hosted every Christmas Eve at one of the large local shelters—since Christmas was an especially tough time for the homeless, she liked knowing they had somewhere welcoming to go on that particular night. *And* it gave her an opportunity to convince newcomers to *stay* at the shelter, where maybe her agency could help them get back on their feet.

He'd gone with her to the dinner the past two years and would this year, too. He loved watching her do her job—she was no less than amazing with the people who wandered into the shelter looking emotionally battered, lost, afraid. Each time he saw her at work it made him fall in love with her a little more.

Although maybe he shouldn't go this year, now that he thought about it. Loving her more would hardly help this situation, which, for him, was growing dire.

"Morning, honey," she'd said.

"Morning, Em." He'd glanced over at her. She was the sort of woman who looked good first thing upon waking, sans makeup, hair tousled.

"I'll be late tonight. Cookie exchange at Lisa's after work." A neighbor friend.

He'd nodded against his pillow. "Maybe I'll do some shopping then."

But so far, he'd managed to buy nothing for her—no gift he could find seemed "right" for right now.

Maybe, he thought then, the idea just striking him as he walked past Victoria's Secret, he should seek out a baby doll nightie like the one in his dream. She'd look gorgeous in something like that.

But then he'd have to beg her to even wear it, and it wouldn't be worth the trouble.

With a sigh—and empty hands—he gave up and headed outside, where it was just beginning to snow.

December 24

I'm going to take a quick shower, sugarplum," Simon said. They'd just gotten home from the annual Christmas Eve dinner at the shelter, where they'd helped serve two hundred and fifty-two homeless people a decent meal. Emily had talked personally to as many as she could, handing out brochures and encouraging them to stay afterward. She would be lucky—and thankful—if thirty or forty took her advice, but if that many people had a better night, and maybe a few of them a better future, that made her efforts more than worthwhile.

And she was fairly exhausted, but not too exhausted to follow through on her plan now that they were home. She and Simon had already developed a few little holiday traditions—and among them was serving dinner to the homeless on Christmas Eve, then coming home and exchanging their gifts to each other. "Okay," she replied. "I'll . . . meet you in the living room in a few. With your present."

She smiled, and he did, too, leaning in to kiss her forehead.

But that didn't change how strange things had been between them lately. As she watched Simon disappear behind the bathroom door, her heart hurt remembering how unhappy he'd continued to seem these past couple of weeks. In fact, she had the distinct feeling that he was "sticking it out" with her until the holidays were over and then might very well be planning to break up.

Every time that thought hit her, it was like a physical blow. And now, with *that* horrible pressure weighing her down, she had to give him the gift she'd been planning—and hope it wasn't too late to save what they had.

She'd followed Dawn's advice to the letter—she'd practiced touching herself, once even doing it in front of the mirror, so she could see what *Simon* would see. She'd grown comfortable with the feel of her own breasts, and even her pussy. She could say that now, and lots of other naughty words, without flinching. Because she'd practiced that, too—dirty talk—also in front of the mirror.

She'd thought herself pretty resourceful when she'd bought Popsicles to simulate sucking Simon's cock. Of course, they were much smaller than what she'd be putting in her mouth tonight, and cold, too—but it had at least allowed her to develop some techniques, and she figured it was better than nothing. And she'd actually reached a place where the idea of taking his shaft between her lips held some appeal for her, some true desire.

So she was as ready as she *could* be.

But she also knew that putting her plans and practice into action would be an entirely different and more complex endeavor. So even though she'd gone through the last two weeks with a smile on her face—at some points truly happy about her new self-discoveries and plans for Simon, at others stressed out and just trying to keep the peace with him until she could complete her "self-education"—her stomach churned and her hands trembled as she went to the bureau to pull out the naughty little outfit she'd bought for this evening.

The shower still ran behind a closed door when Emily once again found herself before a mirror, looking like a December centerfold. Or at least she *hoped* that's how she looked.

She wore a red velvet shelf bra sporting white fur along the top edge, the naughty lingerie built to support her breasts but not to conceal them, so her nipples were fully on display and hard with excitement. Below that, a very short, flouncy, red velvet skirt with more white fur at the hem—and no panties underneath, which had the desired effect of making her feel positively wicked, in a *good* way. Black boots came to her knees and a Santa hat sat perched on her head. *Mrs. Santa Gone Bad.*

She quivered a bit at the sight of herself, with both nervousness and excitement, imagining Simon's surprise at finding his gift already unwrapped and ready to be played with.

Simon ran a towel through his mostly dry hair, then stepped into a pair of underwear and the flannel pants Emily had laid out on the bed for him. Of course, they were dotted with tiny reindeer, ornaments hanging from their antlers. She'd given them to him last Christmas. Why were reindeer becoming such a theme in his wardrobe? But for Emily, he would wear them.

As usual, she'd blown him away at the dinner, and he had, indeed, fallen for her even harder. Maybe it was a foregone conclusion in his life that he was destined to love a woman who hated sex. Starting toward the living room, he let out a sigh. *Why me*?

When he walked through the doorway, Elvis's bluesy, sexy "Merry Christmas, Baby" played low on the stereo, and the room was aglow with candles and the tiny colored lights of the Christmas tree, as well as the low flames burning in the fireplace.

He didn't see Emily—at first.

But when he did, he swallowed. Hard.

What the hell?

She lay stretched provocatively before the decorated tree, amid the gifts, legs slightly bent, back arched, propped on her elbows. Her hands cupped fur-lined breasts, the nipples beaded and shadowy in the dim lighting. *Jesus*. He went hard in an instant.

A big red bow was wrapped around her bared tummy, and her eyes shone on him—Holy Mother of God—with wild intent. He stood before her numb, speechless.

"Do you like your present?" she asked, her voice silky, sensuous—new.

He still couldn't find any words, so simply swallowed again as he nodded.

"Good. Because this is only the beginning."

"Unh," he eloquently managed to reply. His whole body had gone rigid with arousal, but his jaw had dropped and he seemed unable to raise it back up.

Keeping her suddenly sexy eyes on his, she eased both hands up through the fur on her bra to gently tweak the beautifully erect peaks of her breasts. He felt her sensual moves in his cock, yet still wondered just what the hell was going on, what had happened to her. He almost wondered if he was having another dirty dream.

She smoothed her palms over the lovely curves of her velvet-bound breasts and onto her pale torso, where she used her middle finger and thumb to slowly, gracefully pull at the ribbon tied around her waist. He watched, amazed, dumbfounded, as the thick red ribbon gently fell away, giving him the sense that the simple gesture somehow *opened* her to him.

That's when he forgot to keep wondering what was going on and stepped toward her, his feet moving on pure instinct, his body ready to have his way with her—and to hope this was real.

"Stop," she said then, gentle but firm.

He did, but the command caught him off guard.

"Sit." She pointed to the sofa.

"Why?" The first word he'd managed to utter since walking into the room.

She bit her lip, looked slightly pensive for half a second, but then turned all the way sexy again. "I have more to give you, baby. More of *me*."

Once again, Simon swallowed. Emily had always been a beautiful woman, but when—*how*—had she gotten so fucking *hot*? "All right," he said lightly, then did as she instructed, wondering what on earth awaited him.

He watched as she rolled smoothly up onto her knees, then began to crawl in long, sensual strides toward a small ottoman in front of an easy chair situated across from him. The long lines of her legs as she moved so sleekly, the curve of her back, the plump roundness of her breasts, all served to tighten his cock within his pants that much more, and it was all he could do not to bound across the coffee table and ravish her—but he stayed in place, still in wonderment over her gift to him.

She moved lithely up onto the ottoman, facing him, her eyes filled with . . . he could only read it as the deepest passion he'd ever witnessed from her. It wasn't just about *this*, about *sex*. He thought it was about *sex* and *him* and *her* and every moment they'd ever shared together, good and bad.

Then she parted her legs.

He drew in his breath at the erotic vision she made. But only when she reached down, lifting her little skirt to reveal nothing underneath—nothing but the smooth flesh of her shockingly denuded pussy and the pink folds at its center—did a low groan escape him.

"Do you want me to touch myself for you, Simon?"

He nearly fainted. Jesus Christ. "God, yes," he managed on a ragged breath.

Sliding her tongue sensually across her upper lip, and looking coquettish as hell, she reached one long, tapered middle finger down into her glistening cunt. As she raked her finger-tip upward through the valley of pink, they both sighed. He'd never seen a more arousing sight in his life.

"More," he whispered without planning it. That's what he wanted, needed, with his whole soul in that moment. *More.*

Emily complied with his request, her body on fire. She was *doing* this, really doing it, and Simon appeared just as riveted as Dawn had promised he would be. Reaching down, she stroked through her moist flesh for him again and again—each pass drawing another hot sigh or moan from her man even as her own arousal grew.

Having his eyes on her while she did this was more powerful than she'd even imagined. That first stroke had been hard—truly letting go of her lifelong fears about sex was complicated—but now, it was becoming easier, slowly easier, with each swipe of her finger through her moist slit.

Glancing down, she saw how open she was, how excited and ready, and she was reminded of the raw, blatant view she was giving her man. A last ounce of that awful, hideous sense of shame bit at her—but then she forced it away. *This is okay. More than okay. This is good. Pleasuring yourself while you pleasure your lover. This is . . . pretty freaking amazing, in fact.* And then the shame was gone, and she was free. Free to be the woman she wanted to be for Simon.

"You're so hot, my sugarplum girl," Simon cooed to her, his lids heavy now, eyes shaded with desire.

"Do you like this? Like watching me rub my pussy for you?" Her voice came breathy, because it was another step, and felt huge, but she wanted it, wanted to arouse him with her words as much as with her body.

Simon actually looked weak with passion. "Oh my God, baby, *yes*. Rub it for me. Rub your beautiful cunt for me."

She sucked in her breath, more aroused than bothered by the word. Which made a soft smile steal over her face. And gave her even more courage—the courage to follow a whim.

Sensually biting her lip, she reached to a nearby table where a decorative snowman mug held a handful of red-and-white-striped candy canes. She snatched one out, grabbing on to the curve at the end, and slid the length of it slowly through her lips, one side to the other, the taste of the peppermint on her tongue somehow arousing her even more. Then she slowly eased the stick of candy down, down into the folds of her pussy, using it like a finger, surprised when something in the mint made her tingle even more than she already was.

"Aw . . ." Simon moaned, his mouth going slack at the sight.

Emily rolled the peppermint cane slowly across her parted flesh while he watched—before beginning to slide it up and down.

"Oh, baby, that's so fucking hot."

She licked her upper lip, fully into it now, pleasing herself, pleasing Simon. And then she followed another wild whim, letting the tip of the candy cane sink lower, lower, until she held it poised at the opening of her passage. Simon's gaze was glued to her cunt. She eased the length of the candy inside.

Simon's moan cut through the low music that still played, fueling her pleasure, and she followed the instinct to move the thin stick of candy in and out, in and out, pushing it all the way to the crook of the cane, then easing it slowly back for Simon's hungry eyes. She was fucking herself with a *candy cane*. She couldn't quite believe it, but she was fucking herself with a candy cane—and it was good.

So good—the audacity of it, the raw sex of it, the heat that shone in Simon's expression—that she didn't fight the urge to reach her free hand down, using the first two fingers to caress lazy circles over her clit. Mmm, it was swollen now, sensitive and hot—it felt huge beneath her fingers. She moaned in response as the pleasure stretched through her, magnified and multiplied by the motions of the candy cane below and by Simon's rapt attention.

"Make yourself come for me, baby," Simon demanded. And for the first time in her life, she relished a sexual command, feeling the heat of it, the desire it sent spreading through both of them.

She rubbed her clit harder, the circles her fingers made growing faster and more intense, matching the rhythm of the stick of candy she thrust in herself below. "*Mmm,*" she sighed, her pleasure rising, rising.

"Oh yeah, baby. Get yourself off for me. Be my naughty girl." Simon's voice was a low rasp.

Which made her rub herself even harder, quicker. "Mmm, yes," she heard herself purr. "*Yesss.*" So close, so close. *Get there, get there, come for him.*

And just when she began to worry that her fears might come true, that she might not be able to make herself climax—she reached that glorious threshold, that few seconds where she knew she was safe, the orgasm was coming, a heartbeat away.

And then it washed through her, *hard, hard, hard,* in waves of jolting heat that made her clench her teeth and cry out— again, again.

When the waves settled and she came back to herself, she was acutely aware that she was sitting before Simon with a candy cane in her vagina and her fingers wet with her own juices. Now that she'd come, would this all still seem okay?

She met his eyes, wondering if her fear showed as she waited—for his reaction, and for *hers*.

"You," he began, almost seeming at a loss for words, "are *so* fucking incredible."

Her chest heaved slightly with her renewed nervousness. "I am?"

He tilted his head, looking as if she were crazy to ask. "Oh, *baby*," he said. "Come to me. Come to me and let me *show* you how incredible you are."

And that's when Emily knew. It was still all right. She was still excited, even after the orgasm had faded. And she was going to go to him, all right. Only . . .

"No," she said softly, getting to her feet, clutching the freshly extracted candy cane in her hand even as she rounded the coffee table. "There's still more *I* want to show *you,* give *you.* More of my gift to you."

She saw more than heard his sigh as she abandoned the candy on the table, then dropped to her knees between his legs, firmly parting them.

She gazed up at his handsome face. "I want to take you to heaven, Simon." Then she ran the flat of her palm up over the stiff erection making a clear tent in his pants, for the first time *fully* enjoying how hard he was, how big, and that it was all for her. She wanted it.

She wasted no time undoing the drawstring of his pants, pulling them loose, then pulling them down, along with his white boxer briefs. And—*oh!* Talk about *incredible. He* was incredible. She'd never felt such a response to seeing his big, beautiful cock before, but now the mere vision of it ricocheted all through her.

Pulling in her breath, she leaned low, near enough to kiss it, then gazed up at him.

His voice sounded a little choked. "Baby, are you gonna . . . ? Finally?"

"Yes," she whispered, then licked a long path from the base of his shaft to the tip.

He shuddered, and she loved it—but loved even more knowing that she was going to give him what he'd waited for for so long. Although she felt the need to say, "I may not be any good at it."

He let out a cynical laugh, as if she were nuts, and his eyes looked glassy as he peered down at her. "You *can't* be bad at it, honey. It's not possible. You're going to be *perfect.*"

The words echoed through her, giving her the courage she needed, and God knew that the *desire* was suddenly there, suddenly urging her to go down on him, so she didn't hesitate any longer. Taking his cock firmly in her grasp, she swirled her tongue sensually around the head, licking away the moisture there, then she lowered her mouth over him.

Her first thought was—*how do people do this?* It felt immeasurably *huge* filling her mouth. But her second, more pleasant thought was—*oh God, I like it.*

She liked the hot, thready moans that wafted down over her,

she liked the feel of such immense hardness on her tongue, her lips, the inner walls of her mouth. She liked the power she felt there—the power in his cock, and the power *she* held by pleasuring it.

She liked the way his large fingers threaded through her hair, holding it back—just as Dawn had promised. She liked feeling his eyes on her, just as she had when she'd been touching herself for him.

And as she slowly began to experiment, to move up and down, she grew more bold, took him deeper, moved on him more rhythmically—and finally she gained the courage to look up into his eyes.

She'd never seen Simon so fraught with emotion as he said, "See, my sugarplum? Perfect. So fucking perfect."

And she hated that she'd made him wait so long for this, and she hated that she'd wasted so much time not enjoying his large, perfect shaft this way herself.

But then, just as she was sinking more fully into her work, eyes shut, sliding her lips sensually up and down his smooth, steely length, he cupped her face in his hands and eased her mouth upward. "Stop, baby."

She was stunned, and her mouth felt pleasantly stretched as she raised her eyes to his.

"It's too good," he told her, voice trembling. "I don't want to come yet. And if you keep it up . . ."

She bit her lower lip. She didn't want that, either. So she simply nodded and began to climb up into his lap as he lifted her toward him from the floor.

She intended to lower herself onto that majestic erection

now—if she couldn't have it in her mouth, she wanted it in her cunt. But Simon *kept* lifting her, even after she'd straddled him, propelling her upright on her knees.

She gasped when she realized he was sinking *down* on the couch then, bringing his face level with her cunt. Caressing her outer thigh with one hand as he lifted her short skirt with the other, he studied her there, his eyes so close to her bared mound, then shifted his touch, brushing his fingertips over the smooth flesh between her legs. "I can't believe you shaved your pussy," he murmured, looking drunk on the sight.

She couldn't, either, actually. But seeing Dawn that way had inspired her. She'd figured if she was going to do this, let her inner vixen out, she was going to go all the way. Still, she heard herself asking, "Do you like it?"

A low chuckle erupted from his throat. "Oh yeah, sugar-plum. I like it." He cemented the statement by leaning in to place a soft kiss directly on her clit.

"Ohhh . . ." she moaned.

He gazed up at her, eyes ablaze with lust. "Do you want me to lick you, baby? Do you want me to lick your hot little pussy?"

Oh God. Such a dirty suggestion. Yet for the first time, the idea didn't feel too intimate or outrageous. No, it felt just right and was what she wanted more than anything in this moment. "Mmm, yes," she said with a decisive nod. "Lick me."

He groaned at her command, then sliced into her most sensitive flesh with his tongue.

The sensation made her shiver, made her head fall back. "Oh, baby."

"Minty," he said then, on a short laugh. But Emily wasn't even amused. She just wanted more of his tongue.

And—oh yes!—she got it, she got it *so* damn good.

She soon lost track of exactly what he was doing to her—too much pleasure to watch, to take it all in. She felt his tongue dig deep, licking, licking, felt him swirling it around her clit, then sucking intently. Eager fingers thrust up inside her and she moved on them without thinking. The motion thrust her pussy harder against his mouth and he moaned at her enthusiasm.

She soon heard herself crying out, felt her own undulations taking her over. She instinctively lifted her hands to mold her breasts, caress the soft skin there, tease the hard nipples. So much pleasure—everywhere.

But then—oh God—even more. What was *that*? And how was it even possible?

Fresh sensation buffeted her from behind. Her breath began leaving her in harsh, heavy gasps. So good, so very good. That's when she realized, understood—he was stroking the fingers of his free hand over her anus. "Unh . . ." she moaned.

She'd never known something like that could feel so fabulous. She knew about anal sex, but she'd assumed it was just something people did to be extreme—she'd never imagined that area was truly such an erogenous zone.

The pleasure—coming from all sides now—was simply too much. A few seconds longer and Emily could no longer think, reason. All she knew was physical delight, consuming her. She fucked Simon's mouth, his fingers. She licked her lips just to feel something there, missing his cock inside them. She twirled her nipples between her fingertips, pressed her palms harder to her breasts.

"Oh! I'm gonna come," she said, amazed. God, *twice*? This could happen *twice*? But it was—*now*.

"Oh, I'm coming! I'm coming!" she yelled as the orgasm pulled her in completely, pounding through her in hard, rhythmic pulses, shorter but more intense than the first.

The climax left her feeling utterly spent, so as Simon's fingers left her, she sank down into his lap, exhausted. Her arms looped around his neck and his hands rested on her hips, on her little velvet skirt. They smiled lazily at each other—until Simon's expression turned hotter. "Fuck me," he said.

The words didn't even faze her this time. But weariness still gripped her. "I don't know if I can," she said, casting him a well-pleasured grin. "Too tired."

He lowered his chin to scold her. "Oh, you'll *do* it all right, sugarplum. We haven't come this far for you to stop now."

The naughty glimmer in his eye somehow revived her and she lifted her hands to his face to kiss him, realizing she hadn't even done that yet. And she *loved* kissing Simon. As she pressed her mouth to his, their tongues met, and one kiss turned into two, then more. "I love you," she breathed between them, tasting herself on his lips.

"Mmm, I love you, too, Em," Simon growled. "So very much."

And before she knew it, she was rubbing against him, grinding her damp crotch against the hot erection that arced upward across his abdomen. "Fuck me," Simon urged her again, his voice a mere breath now. "Fuck me, baby."

Rising back to her knees, Emily curled her fist around his

cock, positioning herself carefully. One more thing she'd never done—been on top. Her heart beat wildly as she eased down, down, warmly sheathing him in her moisture.

"Oh God," she moaned—he felt so much bigger this way, with her weight on him. She had to clench her teeth for a moment as her body adjusted to the nearly overwhelming pressure.

"You okay?" Simon's hands closed on her waist. "We don't have to do it this way if it hurts."

But Emily shook her head. He was right—she'd come too far to stop now. She knew they could have fun in lots of other new positions she'd never tried, too, but this one was so . . . basic, and so intimate, that she intended to *handle* this, to master it, to not let anything she tried tonight fail. "I just need . . . to get used to it. You're *huge*."

He laughed. "See what you've been missing?"

She smiled into his eyes. "Mmm." Her body was beginning to adjust now, to the feel of him pushing up into her, filling her so impossibly full.

She slowly began to move. And to feel. The way her clit met with his body. The way her pelvis eased instinctively into a gyrating rhythm that felt as natural as breathing.

"That's right," he said, caressing her breasts. "Ride my cock."

Her heated sighs came heavier when Simon dipped to take one breast into his mouth to suckle. The ministrations seemed to connect directly to her pussy and increase the sensation there. Her rhythm on his cock quickened slightly and despite her initial troubles, she already knew why women liked being on top so much.

Simon's hands slid from her fur-outlined breasts downward, up under her little red skirt to knead her ass. "Mmm, that feels nice," she told him, overjoyed at the freedom she felt, with the realization that she was really *doing* this, having fun with Simon, letting her inhibitions run free.

His eyes darkened just slightly as he slid one hand inward, his fingertips brushing over her anus again. She couldn't hold in her moan. "Oh—even better," she purred.

She still couldn't quite get over how that soft little touch in that tiny little spot could spread all through her. It was almost enough to make her weak all over again, yet at the same time, it turned her even more wild, feral, and she found herself kissing Simon feverishly, rubbing her breasts against his chest.

He managed to smile through his heat, though his voice came breathy. "Your fur tickles."

"And what does *this* do?" She rode him harder, amazed she could thrust down so enthusiastically now, feel him so deep inside her cunt without pain.

"*That,* baby, makes me want to fucking explode—so be careful."

Simon continued to stroke across the tiny fissure at her rear, and at moments Emily thought she would lose her mind from the consuming pleasure it sent flashing through her entire being.

Suddenly leaning forward, Simon dipped Emily back over his knees and took the opportunity to lick one sensitive nipple as he reached around her. When he sat back up, drawing her upright again, she saw he'd retrieved her old friend, the candy cane. "Sticky," he said with a grin, holding it up between them.

"Because it's candy or . . . because of me?" she asked, feeling just a hint of sheepishness as she lowered her chin.

"Both," he said, then put the end of the candy cane in his mouth to suck on it.

Mmm, why was that such a sexy sight?

"I taste you," he said.

Oh yeah, *that* was why. Because it had been in her pussy and was now in his mouth.

Which was when he slowly drew it from between his lips, then held it up to hers.

She parted them slightly, letting him slide the candy cane inside. A burst of peppermint filled her mouth, but she, too, tasted the strangely sweet remnants of her own juices, just as she had on Simon's lips moments ago. Her chest hollowed as she gazed into her lover's eyes. He continued slipping the candy cane in and out of her mouth as they fucked, her clit still connecting with him in front as his fingers kept caressing her in back. A whole new wave of weakness set in. She'd never experienced so much passion or true intimacy in her life and was beginning to wonder how women survived it.

So she nearly collapsed when Simon leaned up near her ear to whisper, "I want to fuck your sweet little ass, baby."

Heat climbed her cheeks instantly—a combination of fiery arousal and abject apprehension, the first *real* apprehension she'd felt all night. "Already, Simon? Don't you think we could . . . save that for next time? Because . . . I'm making great strides here, but that's a whole different . . ."

He grinned lasciviously, their faces still close. "Don't worry, sugarplum. I don't mean with my cock. Not yet. You're right, we'll work up to that." He held the candy cane back up between them. "I meant with this."

Emily blinked, swallowed. "Oh." She hardly knew what to think. She wanted to be aghast at the very notion of Simon putting a candy cane up her ass, but she'd just had it in her pussy, so . . . maybe she should just let the man have his way.

Yet he clearly expected her to protest, so his voice came warm again on her ear. "Let me," he said.

Just those two words. But they hit her so hot that she'd have probably let him do *anything* in that moment. "Okay," she agreed.

Raking another warm, sensual kiss across her mouth, Simon deftly reached behind her until she felt the candy—he dragged the dampened end of it up and down in the valley of her ass, teasing her flesh. She sucked in her breath—it made the whole area tingle coolly, the sensation echoing inward. And to her surprise, she found herself moving against it immediately, even as she continued fucking him.

"Be still, baby," he warned her then, and she complied. She leaned in against him, her palms at his chest, her head nestled against his neck where she could breathe in the smell of him— partly shower fresh, partly scented with their sex.

Behind her, the tip of the candy cane slipped inside her anal opening. "*Oh,*" she said.

"Hurt?"

"No." On the contrary.

And she was just on the verge of realizing that her pleasure was starting to expand—greatly—when the candy cane sank home, sliding deep into her ass. "Oh my God!"

Simon looked worried. "Is it okay?"

She could only nod, her whole body filling with a heady, pulsing sensation that stretched all the way to her fingers and toes, even up the back of her neck into her head. "Ah . . . ah . . ." She couldn't speak, could only make noises that probably sounded as if she were stuck somewhere between pleasure and pain, but she was much closer to pleasure. A strange, searing, *overwhelming* pleasure—that only multiplied when she found the strength to move again, to fuck his cock, and in the same motion fuck the candy cane, too.

From there, Emily could barely think—it was too all-consuming. She only knew movement and heat and pleasure and the intense sense of being so fully intoxicated with sensation that she could barely control her actions. She cried out over and over. She heard Simon yell, too. She'd stopped looking at him because her head had dropped back and her eyes had fallen shut. Every nerve ending of her being was pulsing, pumping. Simon's tremendous cock continued thrusting, thrusting, driving up deep inside her pussy, and her clit rubbed against him over and over.

Oh God, God—was she . . . Could she . . . Was it possible to have three orgasms in one night? She'd just begun to wonder when the hot climax rushed through her with more power than any she'd ever known. The shock waves jolted her body over and over—it was like being electrocuted . . . by pleasure.

"Sweet Jesus," she heard herself murmur as finally it passed and she slumped against Simon, her arms falling comfortably around his neck.

"Oh babe," he said. Then louder, "Oh Jesus, babe—*now!*" Extracting the candy cane and tossing it aside, he used both hands to push her hips down onto his cock hard, harder, as he pounded up into her, rocking her body like never before. They both yelled out . . . until again, she was collapsing on him, and this time his body went limp as well, and they sprawled across the couch together, utterly wiped out.

Emily lay on the couch, still in her Christmas Girl Gone Wild suit, recovering from the events of the evening while Simon went to open a bottle of wine. She flung her arms up over her head, smiling lazily. She'd done it, really done it. And it had been more spectacular than she'd ever dreamed.

She sat up when Simon returned carrying two stemmed glasses. He'd kicked off his reindeer pants at some point and was now completely and beautifully naked. For the first time in their three years together, she drank in his male beauty without suffering any shyness.

"To fan-*fucking*-tastic sex," Simon said by way of a toast. His grin was almost enough to get Emily excited again as she clinked her glass against his.

"So," he said after taking a sip, "start talking. What the hell happened to you?"

She bit her lip, tilted her head. "I just realized I *had* to get over my hang-ups if we were going to be happy together."

Simon let out a heavy breath and gave his head a short shake. "I still can't quite believe it, Em. You were . . . astounding. How? How did you get over them?"

She smiled. "That would make a good story for . . . the next time we have sex."

"Like, you mean, tomorrow morning. Or tomorrow night at

the latest. Since tomorrow *is* Christmas and we have families to see and turkeys to eat and presents to open, I might give you the morning off," he concluded with a wink.

She leaned in for a quick kiss. "Tomorrow night—it's a date." Then she glanced at the red stockings hanging on the mantel. "And speaking of presents, I actually have a few more for you. Although only little ones, since *this* was your biggie."

"Trust me, sugarplum, I've never gotten a better gift in my life." He put down his wine and moved toward the fireplace to retrieve both their stockings. Bringing them back to the couch, he sat down and started in on his.

He quickly ripped the red foil paper from the first small gift he pulled out, and Emily saw the edible body paints she'd purchased. "Are those silly?" she asked, wondering now about her choice.

Simon laughed. "No way, sugarplum. Anything that allows me to get more of your body sounds fun to *me*."

"I kinda . . . ventured into a sex shop," she admitted. There weren't many such establishments in the area, but a phone call to Dawn had helped her find one where other women shopped and she didn't feel freakishly out of place. Dawn had met her for lunch and they'd gone together.

"Now *that* I would like to have seen," Simon said with a wink as he extracted his next gift. Removing the paper, he found a DVD featuring Kama Sutra techniques. "Nice," he said. "And from the same store, I bet."

She nodded. "I know I'm doing pretty good here, but I figure we might want to find even more ways to experiment."

His dark gaze met hers. "Absolutely, my sweet girl."

Finally, he opened the last little package stuffed in the stocking—a pair of silk boxer shorts, red with white fur trim and the plastic embellishment of a black belt. She knew she was pushing it with that one, and Simon just shook his head. "Reindeer pants are bad enough, Em, but you really want me to wear Santa shorts?"

She simply nodded, flashing her sweetest "pretty please" expression. She thought them adorably cute.

After a moment, he let out a sigh of concession. "Fine. For you, I'll wear the damn things."

And she smiled. "I'll even let you wear this, too," she added, reaching up to remove her red Santa hat—which had amazingly stayed on through their whole encounter—and placed it on his head. Which was when she realized how hot he looked that way, wearing nothing but the hat. She knew she hadn't managed to hide her lascivious reaction, so she said, "Okay, maybe we can forget the boxers."

He quirked a grin. "That's my newly naughty girl. Ready for *your* present now?"

Again, she nodded, and Simon handed over her stocking. It seemed unusually light, but she hardly cared what was inside. This year had been all about *her* gift to *him*.

Reaching inside, her hand closed around something small and velvet, and she pulled out a miniscule red box. "Hey, this matches my outfit," she said.

Then stopped. And gulped.

Because of what it looked like. A . . . ring box.

She shifted her gaze to Simon's, searching his eyes.

He only gave her a warm smile and slowly said, "Open it."

Taking a deep breath, Emily lifted the lid to find a gorgeous marquise-cut diamond ring inside. And then she lost the ability to breathe at all. "Simon, is this . . ."

When she looked up, Simon had dropped to one knee before the couch. "Will you marry me, Emily?"

All the blood drained from her face. Simon wanted to *marry* her? Even before tonight—before she'd shown him the new, improved sexual her?

She couldn't talk—but she threw her arms around his neck, knocking him backward a bit until he managed to get them both back upright. "Is that a yes?"

She found her voice. "Oh God, yes! Yes, I'll marry you, Simon! *Of course* I'll marry you."

He pulled back, releasing a sigh. "Because, to tell you the truth, I wasn't sure. Lately, things have been . . . weird, and I haven't been . . . very nice."

"Well, who can blame you? I was messing up a major part of our relationship."

He looked her in the eye. "In all honesty, Em, that's really been wearing on me lately, making me question our future together. But no matter how I looked at it, I couldn't give up on us. I knew I wanted to be with you forever, no matter what. And what you gave me tonight . . . I can't tell you how much it means to me."

With that, Simon drew the ring from the box and slid it onto Emily's finger. Gazing down at it, she lifted her other hand to cover her mouth, still stunned. "I can't believe I get such a wonderful man—for life."

He smiled. "*I* can't believe you just fucked my brains out."

She lowered her chin, delivering a seductive look. "There's more where that came from, baby. And you may not even have to wait until tomorrow night. I might just have to have my way with you again right now."

She watched the heat of desire reinvade her lover's eyes and realized, more fully than ever before, how much she'd been missing by letting so much sex with Simon pass her by.

"You know," she said, holding up the hand bearing her new engagement ring, "sometimes the best gifts come in *small* packages. And then, other times," she went on, perusing his whole body, top to bottom, still naked but for the Santa hat, "the best gifts definitely come . . . unwrapped."

.